The Wererat's Tale
Book I: Of Rats & Men
An Abyss Walker Novel

Shane Moore

A New Babel Book release
381 High Point Drive
Holiday Shores, IL 62025

www.ShaneMoorePresents.com

ISBN: 978-1-63196-032-1 (trade paperback)

Third printing.

Printed in the United States of America.

The Wererat's Tale
Book I: Of Rats & Men

Shane Moore

Howard, Shane Moore has created a dark fantasy universe that will rival Tolkien. Grab some popcorn folks! The "Abyss Walker" universe is coming to a city near you!"
  -Michelle Weston, Author of "A Prophecy Forgotten"

"One of the most thought out and in-depth series I have read."
  -Terry Naughton, Disney

"With his Abyss Walker series Shane Moore takes his place squarely in the tradition of fantasy writers the likes of J.R.R. Tolkien and Stephen R. Donaldson. With worlds as much as part of the story as the people who inhabit them, the series seems somehow real in spite of the fantastic happenings that fill the pages. Thick, full prose with characters who come alive on the page make the series a must read."
  -Sean Taylor, Gene Simmon's Dominatrix

"This is definitely going to be the hottest fantasy series to date."
  -Peter Mayhew, Chewbacca from Star Wars

I would like to dedicate this novel to Michael Stackpole. His guidance and tutelage have been invaluable during my career.

1
The Dogs of Night

The glint of the full moon gleamed off of slate rooftops and sliced through the wisps of smoke that floated from the chimneys. Thin fast moving clouds soared over the stone buildings of Central City. The baying of hounds pierced the calm night as they gave chase to unseen prey through the narrow cobblestone alleys.

Demetrin rounded the corner of the alley with Pavicious and Alan right behind him. Their padded boots splashed softly as they ran through puddles that were recently formed from the evening's rainstorm. Sweat glistened on their foreheads and their frantic eyes darted about as the baying of hounds grew louder.

"Hurry" Demetrin growled as loudly as he dared.

The others panted heavily and struggled to keep up with their fleet footed friend. Alan followed close by, but Pavicious lagged behind and he held the side of his fat belly in pain.

"I don't think I can make it much further." Pavicious said in ragged breaths. He leaned against the stone wall of a back street archway.

Demetrin glanced down the alley and back to Pavicious and Alan. He drew his long rapier and jogged back. He could hear the hounds closing in, which meant the city guards were not much farther behind.

"Pavicious, go to Mara. Take her and Kellacun into the sewers. Alan and I will hold them off as long as we can."

Pavicious struggled to get his breath. "What about you guys?"

Alan narrowed his eyes. "It is just a few dogs and guards. As long as the demon elf is not with them, we'll be fine."

Pavicious glanced nervously down the alley. "But Demetrin, how will Mara and Kellacun survive in the sewers? How will I survive? We don't have the gift that you have."

Alan drew his cutlass and stared back down the alley.

"Hurry Demetrin, we have little time for this."

"Roll up your sleeve." Demetrin said as he ran his hands though his short brown hair.

Alan reached in his belt pouch and pulled out several small metal prongs that resembled the child's game of jacks. He tossed dozens of them on the ground around the corner of the alley and backed towards Demetrin and Pavicious. "Hurry up, Pav-co. We can't run with you, your fatness will be the death of us."

Pavicious rolled up his sleeve and glanced nervously as Demetrin started to change. His face twitched as his nose elongated. He gurgled and convulsed as hair erupted from his face and a long rat tail sprouted from the rear of his pants. In seconds, Demetrin had transformed from a spindly rogue into the hybrid form of a half-rat, half-man. His dark black bulbous eyes seemed to penetrate the chubby thief and he recoiled in fear.

Demetrin grabbed Pavicious's bare wrist with his clawed hand and bit down hard. Pavicious tried to wrench his wrist away as blood streamed down his hand and dripped into the wet alley floor. As quickly as he bit him, Demetrin released Pavicious' arm. "Now you will soon have the gift. Go to Mara, take her to the sewers, she will know where to meet me."

Pavicious started to turn when Demetrin grabbed him by his wrist again. "We are all that is left, Pavicious. You must not fail me."

Pavicious took a deep breath and ran down the alley as fast as his stubby fat legs would carry him. Demetrin raised his rapier and started back to Alan.

"Did you bite him?" Alan asked as he stared at the corner of the alley, waiting for the war dogs to arrive at any moment.

"Yes." Demetrin said reluctantly.

Alan shook his head slowly from side to side. "Hope I am wrong about him."

Demetrin did not get a chance to respond, as the dogs rounded the corner. Their dark black coats glistened in the pale moonlight. Several stepped on the sharp metal caltrops. The dogs howled in pain and tumbled to the hard alley floor, but the others charged headlong, growling savagely as spittle sprayed from their mouths.

Demetrin ducked under the first dog as it leapt at his throat and slashed the second with his thin rapier. The animal's neck erupted in a fountain of blood and the dying animal's momentum carried it well passed the two rogues.

Alan brought his heavier cutlass down on the first dog, neatly severing its head, while another beast threw its body into his shoulder, biting him on the forearm. Alan winced in pain as the animal's powerful jaws clamped down on his arm. He staggered back and stabbed the animal in the ribs.

The dog howled and released his bite as he died.

Demetrin ducked and leapt in the air, as he cut down several dogs with his keen rapier. Despite his clumsy appearance, his dexterity was unmatched by their canine foes. Alan stabbed forward and killed another dog when a crossbow bolt whizzed by his head.

"The guards are here, Alan. Mind their bolts!" Demetrin called out as he sliced the throat of another dog.

Alan let out a cry as he was struck in the chest with a heavy crossbow bolt. The thick shaft knocked him from his feet. He fell to the ground and writhed in pain as he clutched the fletching of the arrow.

Demetrin slashed one of the dogs in the throat with his claws and severed the head of the remaining war dog that was trying to bite Alan. His friend was lying on his back

in the alley. Bright red blood dripped from his mouth and the thick gurgling sounds told Demetrin that his friend was soon to be dead.

"Come on!" Demetrin screamed at the city guards that stood at the other end of the alley. "You got no more dogs! Come to your deaths! I will do to you, what the Duke did to the rest of my friends!"

The city guards did not advance. A few were picking caltrops out of their soft leather boots that Alan had left on the ground. Demetrin's keen ears heard a whisper of a sound behind him. He instinctively ducked low, but the lightening fast slash caught him in the back of the shoulder. Pain ripped through his mind and he whirled, slashing his sword at the unseen foe. His rapier was turned aside and Demetrin met the face of his attacker. She was barely five foot tall and had long, silver curly hair that fell out of the cowl of an unusual cloak. Based off of the runes on the cloaks trim she was surely elven, and her sword was like none he had ever seen.

Demetrin could feel the warm wet blood trickling down his back and his sword arm was getting cold and numb. "So, the Duke sends his bitch to deal with me?"

"So you can slay dogs?" she said. "Then it is time to be slain, dog."

Demetrin ducked low as the elf slashed in with unnatural speed and grace. As soon as the blade cleared the thief, she twisted her movements, and side stepped a stab from Demetrin. His blade passed harmlessly by. With little effort, the elf spun, and drew a second sword from under her cloak. She stabbed in with her first blade, forcing the off-balanced Demetrin to parry the strike, while her other sword softy and quietly pierced the wererat under his chin and erupted from the top of his head.

Demetrin felt incredible pressure in his skull and pain under his chin. His eyes bulged and he had difficulty seeing. He soon realized he was on the alley floor and was unable to move. He tried to run, to call out, but soon his fading thoughts drifted to Mara and Kellacun. Then his thoughts were no more.

The small elf wiped her thin blades on Demetrin's cloak. Dark violet blood and brain matter drained from the top of his head and soaked into the cobblestone alley. She stared at Demetrin's body without disgust. "You ran like a rat and died like a dog."

A large man emerged from the crowd of guardsmen as others moved forward and snatched up the two bodies. He was well over six foot tall. He wore a bronze colored skull helm with exaggerated bull horns on the side of it. His well muscled frame was covered in red colored breaches and he held a shield depicting the holy symbol of Stephanis.

"What about the fat one, Ulsta?" the large hunter asked.

The small elf slid a lock of her curly silver hair behind her ear as she sheathed her razor sharp swords. "I suspect that he will lead us back to the rat's home."

"Ulma was there. One of her hunters is waiting in the shadows. There is a daughter that is yet to be accounted for," the hunter said.

Ulsta nodded and motioned to the city guards to carry off the two bodies. "She is following the fat one now. I can sense it. He may lead us to the last remaining thieves, if there are any. If he goes back to the leader's home, then we know we killed them all."

The hunter nodded. "And what of the silver enchanted blades? You have both. Won't Ulma need hers?"

Ulsta shook her head. "No, the leader was the only wererat. He was not nearly the famed swordsman he was said to be. I am a bit disappointed."

The hunter thumbed his large axe that hung at his belt. "And what of the Duke? It is my understanding that he is not a man to be trusted. I have learned that this guild formed when he hired an assassin to kill a mason's guild." "Oh. He did, did he?" Ulsta said.

"Yes, my lady. It seems he contracted a mason's guild to build the coliseum then, when they were nearly finished, they stopped work. It seems he was not going to pay what he promised. When the guild went on strike, he hired an assassin to kill them one by one until they agreed to finish."

Ulsta bit her bottom lip in frustration. "Go on."

"Apparently the mason's banded together and set a trap for the assassin. He was a wererat. The guild leader we killed tonight had been infected by the assassin the night they dispatched him. He then formed the Thieves' Guild to try to punish the Duke for the murder of his friends."

Ulsta thumbed the hilt of her swords. "That explains why they were so difficult to root out. They were not just thieves, they believed in what they were doing."

"So if the Duke backs out on us, how will we get payment from him?" the hunter asked.

Ulsta smiled an evil grin. "We won't. We will do what the mason's were unable to do. We will kill him."

* * *

Pavicious ran through the alleys. He had only been to Demetrin's home once, and he was a bit concerned he would not be able to find it. He knew he was getting close, he had just passed the Beggars' Market.

"So, that elf witch is out tonight," came a voice from the southern market alley.

Pavicious ducked behind some old crates. The only people that knew of the elf were the city guards. He knew they patrolled in pairs of two unless they were giving a woman an escort some place.

Two militia guards emerged from the southern alley. They wore their typical uniform. A plain brown leather jerkin and breaches with a red silk Beyklan cape. They scanned the market to make sure it was closed on time. Often the beggars would sell after the Duke's tax collector had gone home to avoid paying a few copper.

"Yea, I hear she is finishing off the filthy thieves tonight."

"Good riddance." the taller militiaman said as they neared the crates Pavicious was hidden behind.

Pavicious drew his dagger and quietly moved to the far end of the crates. The chubby rogue was careful to avoid the wet puddles from the evening rain. He felt his face flush as the two men spoke of the murder of his friends and family so callously.

"The market is closed, let's head back. I hear Joshua is walking his sweetheart home tonight," the smaller man said.

The taller one laughed, "That pompous fool thinks that serving as a militiaman will make him more normal. I got news for him, his daddy is the Duke. He will never be normal."

Pavicious slid from the side of the crate and felt his disappointment set in as the guards walked away. He slid his dagger back into his belt. The spot on his arm where Demetrin had bit him was starting to itch. He slid his glove up and was surprised to see a large growth of light brown and white hair. The wound was nearly healed, though his glove had a considerably large bloodstain on the underside. Ignoring the odd growth, Pavicious slid out from behind the crate and made his way down the western alley. He did not have to travel far when he came across Demetrin's small shack. *It was odd,* Pavicious thought. *Why would a man who had commanded nearly a hundred thieves and dealt with thousands of gold coins, live in such squalor?*

Pavicious ran to the door of the shack and wiped his sweaty brow. He took a deep breath and when he opened the door, his heart sank.

The shack was in shambles. The furniture had been upturned and everything of value had been broken. Lying in the center of the floor was Mara. She was clearly dead. Her face was swollen and bruised from a severe beating and her body was covered in many small deep cuts. Lying next to her on the floor was the portrait of Demetrin, Mara, and Kellacun. Pavicious remembered when they hired an artist to render it.

Pavicious started to close the door when he felt a sharp stinging pain in his back and another in his front. He tried to call out, but his breath would not come. He stared down in shock and horror to see a shining metal blade that had erupted from his chest. He tried to move, to run, but the blade held him fast. He grabbed at the sword, but his strength failed him and all went black.

Ulma wrenched her sword free from Pavicious. The fat thief fell dead. His heavy lifeless form thudded on the hollow wooden floor of the rundown shanty. The elf's black cadacka floated on the soft night breeze and danced around her shapely form. The silver trim of the cloak seemed like a celestial ribbon hurled about on a stick as she smiled wickedly at the dead body of Pavicious and Mara.

"And then there were none," she said emotionlessly.

* * *

Kellacun and Joshua walked in the cool night air carrying a small brown sack. It was overflowing with breads, grains, and tubers that she had collected just as the market was closing for the day. Father had sent her to task in the evening, but she spent too much time on patrol with Joshua and now she was hurrying home. She glanced up at her wonderful friend. His shoulder length blond hair floated across his face from the soft night breeze. She gazed longingly into his eyes and fantasized about their approaching wedding.

Joshua walked awkwardly next to Kellacun. He admired her unnatural grace as she walked and often wondered if she was secretly one of the traveling circus performers his father often spoke of. He had never been so enthralled with a woman before. Sure, he had attracted several glances daily from the ladies in waiting, but he found himself smitten with a poor mason's daughter. She was a raging beauty that seemed to have an inner fire that could not be quenched.

"Please let me carry those for you, Kellacun." Joshua asked earnestly. "I feel like a miscreant walking next to you.

It's the man's duty, you know?"

She flashed a wry smile and smirked. "I'm doing fine. You shouldn't try to pamper me. Papa taught me to stand up for myself and that no matter what, right is right and wrong is wrong."

Joshua scratched his head. "So, how is carrying your groceries wrong? I mean, I want to help out."

"Help me when I need it, silly. Not when I am capable to doing it on my own."

"Your father sounds like a fine man, I am nervous about meeting him."

Kellacun paused in the cool alley and turned to face Joshua. He was much taller than she, and she loved him for it. She liked how his wind blown hair danced across his face.

Joshua quickly snatched her up in a passionate kiss. Kellacun exhaled softly and slowly lowered the sack of groceries before dropping them to the alley floor. She placed her hands behind his head and wove them into his golden hair. She pulled away from the kiss and placed her forehead to his, biting her bottom lip with a vixen's smile. "I will have you on our wedding night, Joshua. I will take you for my own."

Joshua chuckled uneasily. "I am supposed to be the one doing the taking and the having, buttercup."

"Can't you handle a strong and fierce woman?" Kellacun asked as she nibbled his bottom lip.

"Of course," Joshua answered. "But, I want to spoil you.

Treat you like the princess you are."

Kellacun averted her eyes and started picking up the sack. Her smile faded and she became quiet.

"What's wrong, my love?"

Kellacun looked up as she placed the tubers into the sack. "My family is poor, Joshua. I am afraid you will judge me a guttersmug."

"A guttersmug!? You could be no worse than an alley urchin," he said jokingly. "Do not fear, my love. My family makes more than enough money for the both of us. We shall be living high on the hog at the keep as soon as it is built."

Kellacun finished picking up the groceries. "That sounds so nice. Strawberry kisses in the morning and pears for lunch. No more blasted tubers!"

Joshua smiled. "We can even move your parents in, once the Torrent Manor family estates is finished. Father says they are building a southern wing that will have a worship area and family living apartments. It will be one of the
grandest keeps ever constructed!"

Kellacun smiled and shook her head. "No, my father is a proud man, he would never give up his business."

Joshua nodded as he began to survey their surroundings. "How much farther? We are nearing a danger area. My father has the hunters out."

Kellacun glanced into the shadows fearfully. She had heard her father talk of these cold blooded killers. If they suspect that you were even with the Thieves' Guild, they would cut you up and torture you. "It's not too much farther."

As the pair rounded the alley corner, Kellacun spied her home. It was a small adobe shack nestled amid a bunch of larger run down buildings. Her mother had taken care to keep the street sludge away from their home, but the general stench of poverty hung in the air.

"There it is." Kellacun offered.

Joshua felt his heart sink. He scanned the buildings and the alleys in hopes that he was mistaken.

"What is it?" Kellacun asked.

Joshua frantically snatched Kellacun by the shoulder, wrapped his forearm around her neck, and pulled her into the alley. "Kellacun, no!"

Kellacun stared back at Joshua awkwardly and wrenched herself fee from his grasp. She glanced back into the alley to see if some threat was there, then readjusted her hair. "What is wrong with you, Joshua?"

"Kellacun, my love. My sweet, sweet, Kellacun," Joshua said softly. "There is something you must know."

"What is it, Joshua? Don't be foolish."

Joshua wiped the rapidly forming sweat from his brow and double checked no one was coming down the alley.

"My love, is your father named, Demetrin?"

Kellacun smiled uneasily. "Yes. He is a mason. You know that. And my mother's name is Mara."

Joshua ran his hands though his hair nervously and took Kellacun by the shoulders. He led her to a crate in the alley and pushed her back gently, forcing her to sit.

"Joshua, what is it? Stop being silly. I'm a grown woman. You can tell me anything. Is my home too poor for you?" she asked, readjusting her blouse.

Joshua ran his hands through his hair and paced in the

alley, checking time after time to see if anyone was coming. "Kellacun, your father was listed as one of the Thieves' Guild and was to be arrested tonight. I know, because they gave us a briefing on what areas to avoid, that the hunters would be out."

Kellacun erupted from her seat and started down the alley.

Joshua tried to reach out and catch her, but the young woman's superior speed easily avoided his grasp.

"Kellacun, wait! They will kill you!"

Kellacun ignored his warning and burst through the door of her home. The small shack was in shambles. Furniture had been overturned, decorations smashed, and laying on the floor was the crumbled body of her mother. "No!" she screamed as she ran across the room, stepping over debris and the body of Pavicious. She stopped as tears streamed down her face. Dropping to her knees amid the blood and broken debris, she lifted her mother's head. Bruises covered her once beautiful face and her body was swathed in many small cuts signifying she had been tortured. Kellacun held her mother to her bosom and wept.

Joshua ran into the room with his sword drawn. His warm breath fogged around his mouth in the cool night air.

"Careful Kellacun. The hunters could still be out."

Kellacun rocked back and forth, holding her mother to her chest. "Why Joshua?" she cried. "My family were not murderers. They were masons! They did not deserve this!"

Joshua felt his heart sink. He struggled to find his voice, but could not find the strength to answer.

"Oh mama!" Kellacun wailed.

Joshua started toward her when a movement in the shadows caught his eye. He turned to see the hulking form of a hunter's helm in the shadows. Its double bull horns cast an eerie shadow on the dark, unlit wall of Kellacun's shack.

"Kellacun, my love. We must leave. Now!"

Kellacun turned. "Why? My family is dead. Do me the mercy and strike me down too since we are so vile in your eyes!"

Joshua hurried forward with his sword drawn. "I am Joshua Dean Blackhawk, son of Duke Dolin Blackhawk and

I command you to stand down!"

Kellacun turned to see a shadow erupt from the darkness. It was a massive, hulking form that shook the shack as it charged forward. Kellacun fell backwards in shock and raised her hand in defense.

Joshua brought his sword up from low and met the heavy axe that the hunter had brought down. The two blades met in a tremendous ring that echoed in the tiny shack. "Kellacun, run!"

The hunter punched forward and caught Joshua in the face. The stunned guard staggered back, narrowly deflecting a second deadly axe slice.

Kellacun glanced at the door and then back at the scene before her. She could not leave Joshua. She franticly scanned the room for a weapon when her eyes fell on the crumpled form of her mother. Kellacun felt her self drifting away. She was transported to another place, another mind. She felt a fire welling up inside of her. He vision blurred and her face went numb. She felt angry and powerful.

Joshua was struck with another bone crunching blow to the face. His vision blurred and he raised his sword in defense. A sharp pain tore into his arm and his hand went numb. He staggered back in shock as his severed hand and sword fell to the floor.

Kellacun erupted from the doorway. She felt herself gliding across the floor with unnatural speed. The hunter turned and Kellacun hurled herself into the chest of the monster. The force of the blow knocked the massive man into the wall and then through it. He fell into a mass of broken wood and rocky debris. Kellacun turned and saw poor Joshua. He struggled to stop the bleeding from his hand. He was pale white and had lost a lot of blood. "Wrap it, Joshua. If you lose too much blood, you can die."

Joshua staggered to his feet. He wrapped a torn cloth bandage around the nub and fought to remain conscious.

"Where is the hunter?"

Kellacun glanced back at the hole in the wall of her shack and the hunter's axe lying amidst the rubble. "He is down for now, but we need to flee."

Before she could go any further, the wall next to them exploded in a cloud of dust and debris. Kellacun felt a vice like grip around her neck as her body was hoisted into the air and hurled across the room. She struck the far wall hard and landed on the blood soaked floor. Joshua tried to step towards her, to help her, but fell to the ground. He weakly pulled a dagger from his boot. The silver bladed weapon had been given to all of the guardsmen to defend against the wererat thieves.

"Kellacun!" he shouted weakly and slid the dagger across the floor.

Kellacun was dizzy and her head was foggy. She weakly grabbed the dagger that lay next to her as the hunter grabbed her long black hair. She felt herself being dragged across the floor. She struggled to break loose, but her bruised body only twitched in protest.

"Get away from her!" Joshua yelled as he hurled a rock at the hulking mass of a man.

The rock struck the hunter in the shoulder. He turned with an emotionless stare from behind the skull faced helm. The bull horns seemed to point at Joshua like the tip of a sword. The hunter dropped Kellacun and picked up his axe. His forearm muscles gleamed in the pale light from the damaged wall.

Kellacun glanced up to see the monster walking toward Joshua. Rage filled her again. Her vision blurred and her extremities numbed. With renewed power and vigor she leapt through the air and slammed the dagger deep into the back of the hunter. The blade sunk to the hilt. The hunter arched his back in pain and turned, striking Kellacun with a powerful backhand. The blow knocked the lighter woman against the far wall and into the cabinet. Dishes and glass crashed around her. But as soon as she hit the floor, she was up and charging back. Her eyes were red with fury and her skin was covered in a dark black fur. A long dark tale trailed behind her as her once beautiful features faded away and were replaced by those of a rat.

The hunter growled and charged forward. The two combatants met in the center of the room. Kellacun ducked a slash and stabbed her dagger into the ribs of the hunter, while stepping onto his knee. Her clawed feet dug into his flesh as she maneuvered up onto his body.

The hunter slashed and swung several times as Kellacun ducked and dodged, stabbing in with her dagger and hitting home. The hunter was bloodied and weak, but did not let out any sound of pain.

Joshua rubbed his eyes. "Kellacun…?"

She did not respond. She stabbed the hunter again, and again. The dying man fell to his back in the small shack. Kellacun quickly jumped over him, stabbing again and again. Great gouts of blood slung through the air like a punctured waterskin. Joshua stared in horror at the scene that played before him. His friend, his love, his Kellacun was one of the very rat monsters that had been killing his friends and family.

Joshua struggled to his feet and staggered out of the door of the tiny hovel.

Kellacun stabbed, bit, and slashed the hunter long after he had stopped moving. She heaved in labored breaths and sat atop the mutilated form of her enemy. She glanced around the room for Joshua, but she could not see him. Kellacun was amazed at how well she could see in the dark. It was as if the moon had tripled in brightness. Though her new vision granted her little color, she could see much more than before.

Kellacun got up from the hunter and slid the dagger into her boot. The hand that held it was burning and she glanced down to find that she was covered in a black fur. The wererat held both of her arms in front of her and shrieked when she saw they were covered in fur too. She ran to the door and stuck her head out into the cool night air. "Joshua!" she screamed out. The only sound that answered was the barking of dogs and the angry commands from their masters to quiet down.

Kellacun stepped back into her home in shock. *What have I become?* She thought to herself. She walked back into the room and kneeled above the smashed and blood soaked portrait of her family. A tear dripped down from her hybrid face. Her sorrow was interrupted by the shouts of men. She glanced at the door Joshua had ran through and then at the hole in the wall that led to the cool embrace of darkness. Kellacun silently slipped through the hole and into the maze of Central City's alleys.

* * *

Joshua staggered down the alley back the way he came.

"Help! Guards!"

The sounds of voices and shouts answered back as Joshua slumped to the ground just outside of Kellacun's home. Within moments several militia guards ran up. Their long red capes fluttered in the night. One of the men knelt down and began to tend to Joshua's arm while the others entered the shack with their weapons drawn.

"Stephanis's ghost! What happened?" One of the guards asked.

"There is a dead hunter in here. Someone killed a hunter!" Another answered.

Soon several more guards came running up. They began to search the inside of the hovel and around the outside of it. A man with brown hair and a light beard knelt in front of Joshua. He was wearing brass colored scale mail and his long flowing cape enveloped the ground where he knelt.

"Joshua, it's me. Sergeant Thorrin. Are you ok?"

Joshua weakly opened his fluttering eyes. "Oswald?"

"Yes, Joshua. It's me. Who killed the hunter? Did you kill it?"

Joshua turned and glanced back at the shack and then back to Oswald. "No. It was something else."

Oswald glanced back down the streets and alleys nervously. "Something else? Was it human?"

Joshua fought back the tears that were beginning to well up in his somnolent eyes. "I don't know what it was,

Oswald. Just get me to a healer."

2
Of Rats and Men

Small wisps of thin black smoke danced and twirled in the afternoon wind from a large unfilled grave. Dozens of half burned-half rotted bodies of men and women laid in a twisted pile of death. Some of the bodies were partially covered in dirt. Three men wearing the militiaman guard of Central City stood above and appraised the pit. They carried a large handcart behind them that was piled with three more bodies. The stench of death hung in the air like a fog. The guards adjusted the cloth they used to cover their nose and mouth. Scavenger birds hovered above and below, feasting on the free meal that was left open for weeks.

The men emotionlessly dumped the bodies from the cart into the pit. The corpses tumbled down and came to rest near the bottom. Several crows leapt up to avoid the fresh bodies and quickly landed again to assess their new feast. The guards turned and started back toward Central City without emotion.

Pavicious opened his eyes and glanced around. He was lying amid the rotten and burned bodies of the mass grave. He quickly checked his chest and giggled quietly when he discovered the wound had healed.

Ignoring the putrid swollen corpses of his friends, Pavicious climbed over the bodies and out the far end of the mass grave. The fat thief quickly removed his shirt and tossed it back among the dead and made his way into the forest.

He walked for several hours, ignoring the biting insects and humid summer Beyklan air. After several hours of marching, he crested a hill. At the bottom, Pavicious spied a small farm. The home was made of wood and thatch that had a thin brick chimney on the far end. Chickens clamored about the yard and a few small cows grazed in a poorly maintained pasture just outside of the tiny barn.

Pavicious made his way down the hill, moving from tree to tree. He scanned around the barn and home for signs of dogs, but did not see any. A dog was the last thing a thief wanted to encounter. He silently made his way to the edge of the barn and quickly slid inside the cracked door. The interior of the barn was a mess of broken farm tools and poorly maintained implements. There were two stalls that probably held the livestock and a pile of moldy hay in the back corner.

The chubby rogue made his way to an old water barrel and picked up a pair of ragged breeches and a torn jerkin. Though they were not quality clothing, they were better than the pants he had on. They were covered in rotted filth of the mass grave. Pavicious removed his old clothes and slid into the ones from the barrel. They were a little damp, but their coolness was refreshing to his sweaty skin. When he picked up the breeches, a small dirk fell from the pocket and landed on the straw strewn barn floor.

He smiled at his luck and picked up the knife after slipping into the breeches. They were a little too snug for him, but the portly thief figured he would make do.

Pavicious glanced around for something to eat when the side door to the barn popped open. He instinctively jumped back as an elderly man came in with a small axe in his hand. He was wearing a dark brown tunic and an oversized straw hat.

"What the hell you doin' in my barn?!" The farmer screamed.

Pavicious backed up with his hands up defensively. "Nothing, sir. I was just going."

The farmer narrowed his eyes and his wrinkled face creased in an angry scowl. "You better be getting me feeding clothes off if you want to leave this barn alive."

Pavicious continued to back towards the open door and started to reach for the dirk. The farmer sensed he was going for a weapon and closed in. He swung the hand axe over his head. Pavicious tried to duck the blow and raised his hand up defensively. The sharp weapon cut deep into his arm knocking the fat thief back into the wall. "Damn thief!"

Pavicious ignored the pain in his arm and lunged forward with the dirk. He felt it hit home into the frail old man. The sharp blade pierced his ribs, making a crunching sound. His eyes went wide and the farmer collapsed to his knees. The small axe fell to the straw of the barn floor as the old man slid from the blade.

The farmer slowly rolled to his back as bright red blood gurgled from his mouth and ran down the sides of his cheeks. His eyes were wide with terror as he reached out to Pavicious pleading for help. The fat thief ignored the dying man and stepped over his pleading form, marveling at the rapidly healing axe wound on his forearm. "I have it! I have the gift!"

Pavicious ducked from the barn and disappeared into the forest towards Central City while the farmer choked to death on his own blood.

* * *

Joshua stood among many men in a large marbled room. Thick Beyklan tapestries hung down from the walls of the chamber depicting men battling orcs. Their bright red and white backgrounds were in stark contrast with the bright green orc enemies that were depicted on them. There was a half moon oak table in the center of the room filled with nobles that were adorned with jewelry and self imposed titles and importance. In the center of these nobles was Duke Dolin Blackhawk.

He was an intimidating man with long black hair that was streaked with an occasion lock of silver. His face was wrinkled with derision as he glared at his son that stood before him. In the far corner a small framed woman leaned against the wall. Her arrogant posture and sleek black cloak made her stand out in the room of nobles and their flashy colors. Her long silver hair hung down out of the cowl and covered the front of her sleek leather black bodice. Joshua eyed the cloak suspiciously. It was trimmed with silver lining that was littered with odd looking black runes. He surmised it was some sort of elven writing.

"I assume you have your report ready, Joshua?" the Duke asked with an arched eyebrow of disapproval.

Joshua shot an angry glare toward the diminutive woman and then back to his father. "I do, Duke." he said, adding emphasis on his father's title.

The Duke gritted his teeth. "Well?"

Joshua pointed at the elf with his blood soaked bandage of his severed hand. "Her hunter attacked me!"

Ulsta folded her arms under her breasts and chuckled.

"If my hunter attacked you, then you would be dead." Joshua kicked at the table.

"I killed the murdering monster!"

The room erupted in quiet mumbled talk as Ulsta pushed off of the wall and strode towards Joshua. Though she was barely five foot tall, her presence seemed to dominate the room. She walked right up next to him and stood inches from the angry man. "There were no murders, you fool boy. There were executions. Orders from your father. His orders were carried out swiftly and completely. The Thieves' Guild is no more. I and my hunters eliminated it in a mere week, what the city was unable to do in ten."

Joshua glared and slammed his bloody nub down on the table. Bright red blood began to soak into the white bandage from the aggravated wound. "Her soldiers attacked me. I am living proof that her methods of eliminating this threat are radical and wicked! How are we to know that her men did not murder townsfolk and then created wild tales of half-rat and half-men to scare our nobles into paying her!?"

Duke Blackhawk erupted from his chair, knocking it over backwards behind him. He pounded his fist into the table and leaned forward shaking his finger angrily at his son. "I don't care if you're my son! To level accusations against those in my charge are the same as leveling accusations against me! You are excused, Joshua!"

Joshua snarled and turned towards the door, intentionally bumping into the smaller elf. As he reached the door, he opened it and turned back to the room. "I will get to the bottom of this, father! This wicked elf has killed more than thieves, and she will pay for it!"

* * *

Kellacun rushed out the back door of her family's shack. She could hear the shouts of soldiers and the baying of hounds as they neared her home. She glanced down at her fur and clawed hands as tears streamed down her cheeks. What had she become? She ran faster than she had ever run before. It felt as if the mere tips of her feet touched the cold alley floor. With a leap, she scampered up the guttering of a small hovel and bounded across the slate shingles. Her soft boots made little sound as she leapt from the roof across the alley and to a higher roof on the other side.

She continued to leap and climb, reaching the highest buildings of Central City. Kellacun finally stopped to rest on a small window perch of the dwarven civic building. She slid to her butt and cried as she carefully laid down the blood stained portrait and silver dagger. Her hand burned where she held it, though she did not show any injury. She marveled at the fine smooth black hair that covered the back of her hand and the sharp black claws that tipped her fingers. What had she become? Was she a rat monster that her father had warned her about?

How could Joshua have lied to me? Kellacun thought to herself. *What was that monster in my home? And what kind of monster have I become?*

Kellacun placed her furred head in her hands as she felt her body tingle. She glanced down at her hands as the hair fell away from her body. Her sharp black fingernails retreated back and in moments, she looked as she did before she transformed.

She wiped her tear streaked face with her sleeve as she picked up the family portrait. If her mother was dead, then her father was surely murdered too. She gently removed the blood soaked wooden frame and slid the portrait into her pack before reaching down to pick up the silver dagger that Joshua had given her. But when she picked up the small dirk, hot stinging pain erupted in her hand. She dropped the weapon to the hard slate tile that covered the roof.

Kellacun glanced at her hand and did not see any marks. Confused she reached down and lightly touched the dagger. She felt white hot pain erupt from her finger as if she were touching one of her mother's scalding soup pans. Kellacun pulled her finger away and was surprised to see that she was not hurt.

She repeated this process, but kept her hold on the dirk longer and longer, yet each time, she was not injured. After several minutes, she steeled herself and picked up the silver blade letting the weapon sear her hand. Kellacun reveled in the pain, knowing that it was the knife given to her by Joshua. The knife that he was issued to kill her parents if he happened across them. The knife of betrayal that burned her heart.

After several seconds, she neatly tucked the blade in her belt and slid to the edge of the roof. Her soft boots slid smoothly against the slate tile until she came to a seated position above the alley floor below. She sat for a moment as her feet dangled over the edge.

How much did Joshua know? Is there no person left in my life I can trust? Kellacun thought to herself as the light evening wind blew her dark hair about her face.

She deftly rolled to her belly and climbed down the water spout to the alley floor. She wanted to curl up in a ball and cry, but the anger fueled by the pain of her lost parents drove her onward. Kellacun moved from one shadow to the next, ducking behind old crates and water barrels as she moved through the streets. The young rogue decided that she needed to find Joshua and see if he was okay. She was lost and confused with no where to turn.

Kellacun made her way to the large domed building of city hall. The structure was large, more than six stories high. Its gutter work and roof was topped with bronze, giving the structure a kingly look in the dark night. Kellacun had spent several nights at the palace when Joshua had snuck her in. Though she had never tried to sneak in herself, she had been forced to climb from the window one night when his father had burst into the room. She recalled being terrified that evening, but after she made her way along a ledge, she climbed down the draining spout. After she was home, she thought the whole endeavor to be exciting.

Kellacun ducked past two guards standing outside the entrance to the city civic building. They were not the normal city guards she was accustomed to seeing. They wore brass colored scale mail and had long flowing red capes. They were more muscular than the typical city guard and they scanned the night with hawk like eyes. Their shields bore the symbol of Stephanis, the God of Justice. Kellacun inched closer in the shadows to hear what they were talking about.

"Did you hear the elf managed to kill all of the thieves?"

"Yea, she killed the last few in the alley. A fat one named Pav-co, and the rat leader, named Demetrin. I hear she ain't natural, plus she has those hunters too."

"I heard that too. Like she has some kind of magical powers, like a wizard or something. "

"Wizard? I was thinking more like a demon!"

Kellacun felt her heart sink and her rage build. *Demon?*

I will show that bitch of a demon! she thought to herself. Kellacun could feel her skin begin to tingle and her nose started to numb. She knew immediately that she was beginning to transform and she focused her thoughts to try to keep the beast down. After several minutes, she succeeded in suppressing the change.

When she was satisfied she would not transform, Kellacun moved back into the alley and started climbing the gutter spout. She marveled at how much easier it was now, than a few months ago. Her hands just seemed to fit in the nooks just right and her toes always seemed to find the right hold on the first try. Normally it would have taken her several minutes to climb a spout of this height, but now, she had scampered up the thin bronze guttering in seconds.

Kellacun reached the top of the structure and stepped onto the same narrow ledge that she had to sneak around that night when she was with Joshua. It seemed much wider than she remembered and she easily moved alongside it. The young rogue was not sure which window she needed, so she just entered the first one. She silently dropped down into the hallway and ducked behind a large potted plant.

The hall was lined with a bright red carpet that spanned only the center of the floor. She knew this was to allow the guards to move around the palace at night without their boots clunking on the stone floor. This told Kellacun she was near the sleeping rooms, and most likely near Joshua's room.

The sights and the smells of the palace seemed to warm her heart. As she strained her eyes to see in the darkness, she spied a set of large double doors. They were nearly ten feet high and bore an ornate carving of Stephanis on them. Two palace guards were posted outside of the door. Both were snickering at something and Kellacun could hear loud voices from inside. She snuck from behind the plant to one of the heavy red tapestries that hung from the wall to hear what was being said on the inside of the room.

"I don't care if you are my son! To level accusations against those in my charge is the same as leveling accusations against me! You are excused, Joshua!"

"I will get to the bottom of this, father! The wicked elf has killed more than thieves and she will pay for it!"

Kellacun could hear the heavy footsteps nearing the door. She glanced around frantically for somewhere to hide, but if someone were to come near her, she would be seen easily. Kellacun spied several thick wooden rafters that were neatly tucked in the dark about fifteen feet about the floor. Without thinking, she leapt up to one that spanned the hallway. She was amazed at how high she jumped, but was unable to give it much thought when Joshua emerged through the double doors.

He was clearly angry, but his features warmed her heart. The bandage over his severed hand pained her, but the joy of seeing him overcame any pain she had. Joshua stormed down the hall toward Kellacun and walked directly under her. She turned quietly and then leapt to another rafter as he moved through the palace hall.

Joshua rounded the far corner and Kellacun dropped down to the carpeted floor. She was as silent as an evening breeze using her long legs to displace the force of her fall. Joshua fumbled with the keys to his room and Kellacun ran down the soft carpet with her head low. She felt faster than she had ever been. She seemed to hear everything that was around her, she could smell the sweat and anger on Joshua's brow and she could hear the chuckling of the guards down the corridor that they came.

Joshua opened the heavy wooden door to his chambers and slid through. He turned to close the door and Kellacun leapt like a powerfully coiled spring. She hit him in the chest with her shoulders, wrapping both of her arms around his waist. The force of the blow carried them both into Joshua's chambers and they landed on a soft plush crimson rug. Joshua felt cold steel placed against his neck and a small, but powerful figure was resting on top of him as he lay on his back.

Kellacun glanced around the room briefly as she ignored the white hot burning pain from holding the silver dagger. It was as fanciful as she recalled. The room was adorned with tapestries and fine polished oak furniture. His bed was large and tall with a thin canopy sheet. She doubted he ever would need to use it since every window in the palace was covered in glass. Kellacun glanced over at the window near the far wall that she had ducked out of that time his father came into the room unannounced. Those were good times.

"Are you going to sit atop of me rogue, or are you going to ask me where my valuables are?" Joshua growled.

Kellacun lowered her face closer to his in the pale light of the evening moon. "I don't think you value anything but

your father's villainous plots."

"Kellacun?" Joshua stammered. "Is that you?"

"You knew my parents were to be murdered, didn't you?" Kellacun pressed the dagger tighter against Joshua's neck. "Tell me, lover. Why don't I kill your betraying ass?"

"What are you talking about? I feared you were dead."

Joshua stammered. "What happened to you?"

Kellacun narrowed her bright blue eyes in the darkness of the room. "You should be fearing your own death this night, my love."

Joshua relaxed and let his head fall flat against the crimson rug. "Let me explain, Kellacun. Then if you don't believe me, I'll not stop you from killing me."

Kellacun snapped to her feet quickly and sheathed her dagger as she still loomed over Joshua. When he did not move, she stepped to the door and quietly closed it.

Joshua sat up slowly and rubbed his neck.

"So, are you one of the murderers in the Thieves' Guild? The ones that threatened my father's life and killed many of the charnisseurs?"

"Neither my father, or his men, ever killed anyone that was not trying to kill them." Kellacun knew only of her father's fights as a mason. She slowly walked back toward Joshua. "My father may have been many things, but my mother and I are innocent. It was your father that had them murdered like dogs. You knew this was happening, what other lies have you told, my love?"

Joshua snarled as he got to his feet. "Lies? This is ridiculous! I love you!"

Kellacun kicked Joshua in the chest, knocking him back on the bed, tearing the canopy screen down on top of him. "Do you? Or was that just a ploy to get close to my family?"

Joshua ripped the transparent canopy sheet from his head. "Lies!? How about your lies, Kellacun? You did not tell me your family was responsible for murdering my father's men! Or that you were one of the rat monsters yourself! Tell me, how many men have you killed?"

Kellacun was stunned. Was she a rat monster? She had transformed, but how? Why? "I am not one of the rat people. I… I don't know what happened."

Joshua stood up and angrily tossed the canopy skirting to the floor. "You're not? Why do you think that dagger hurts you when you touch it? My father issued those to us to protect every one of his men from the rat-folk. We were told that silver is the only thing that hurts them."

Kellacun thumbed the pommel of the silver blade and winced as it burned her finger.

"See? The silver burns." Joshua said as he pointed to the blade. "How many other rat-folk are left?"

Kellacun did not answer. She hurried to the window and opened it. The cool night air rushed into the room. "I love you, Joshua, but I'll not let my family's murder go unavenged. My father may have been a thief, but my mother and I were innocent."

Joshua felt his tone soften and he reached for Kellacun's shoulder. Her once pretty outfit had been ruined from the fight and from her change. Kellacun jerked her shoulder away from his touch. "Don't turn away from me, Kellacun. Maybe we can cure you?"

Kellacun turned in a fury. Her bright blue eyes swirled with anger. "My abilities, handed down from my father, are not a disease to be cured. It is a gift. A gift that I will use as a power to avenge his death." Kellacun hopped up into the window sill and turned to face him.

Joshua recoiled at the anger and hate that dripped from Kellacun's tone. "I'll not let you kill my father,

Kellacun. He is a good man that was stopping wicked lawlessness."

Kellacun drew the silver dagger from her belt and pointed it at Joshua. She ignored the hot stinging pain as she

held it. "And I'll not sit idly by while the leaders of this fine city commit murder."

"Murder, my love? There were murderers, but they have all been dealt with."

"No my love, there are two murderers that have yet been brought to heel." She said as she leapt from the ledge.

Joshua ran to the window in time to catch a glimpse of Kellacun's shadowy figure leaping from rooftop to rooftop. "Kellacun, don't throw away your life!" he called out before trialing off into a whisper. "Don't throw away our love."

3
The Heart of a Rat

Pavicious made his way through the night time alleys of Central City thumbing the heavy purse he just lifted from a drunken merchant. He was not sure if he should avoid guard patrols or not, so he erred on the better side of caution. The cool night air forced him to rub his chubby arms on several occasions and he wished he had stolen more clothing from the old farmer.

As he made his way to the area of Central City that was a haven for scum and villainy, he double checked that his dirk was well concealed and entered into a rough and tumble bar known as The Gut. Dozens of eyes fell on Pavicious, and then quickly fell away. These were not folk that needed to stare. Most had sized him up and or recognized him with a glance. Their lives depended on their ability to quickly assess a man, and Pavicious finally felt at home.

He made his way through the tables and chairs. Patrons played cards, dice, and arm wrestled for sport, but all of them kept a sideways glance in his direction. He could feel their eyes on him as he approached the bar. He climbed atop a stool and tossed a few copper coins he lifted from the street onto the table.

"I see Demetrin's chub boy managed to survive the hunters." the bar keeper said as he washed out an old wooden mug and filled it from the tap. He slid it to Pavicious and then pocketed the coins.

"Yea, seems I owe that bastard Blackhawk a good poking from my sword." Pavicious replied as he took a deep draw from the mug.

The barkeeper chuckled as he tossed his wet rag on the counter and leaned forward. "Ha! Good one, Pavco. You ain't got nothing but a cheap dirk tucked under your belt and some undersized farm clothes. How do you suppose you will do anything now that the guild is broken?" Pavicious finished his drink and slammed the wooden mug down, scooting it towards the bar keeper. He tossed a few more copper coins on the counter. "I got some plans. The stupid watch think me dead. I can work anonymously now. No guild, no tithes, all money in my pocket."

The barkeeper refilled his mug and slid it to him, placing both of his hands on the counter again and leering forward. "Don't get too excited, fatty. A few of Spot's guys have been forming a little guild themselves."

Pavicious shrugged his shoulders and took a deep draw.

The bar keeper sighed and started wiping the counter.

"Although, Spot's guys don't have the connections that Demetrin had, they don't have his abilities either."

Pavicious finished the mug and belched lightly. He wiped his mouth with his sleeve and tossed more copper coins onto the bar. "A guild, huh?"

"Well, more of a gang. But since Demetrin fell out of favor and the Duke betrayed him, none of the fellows wants to try to make a deal for fear of the same result. When the Duke brought in the devil bitch, all ideas of deals went out the window." The barkeep refilled the empty mug.

Pavicious took his fresh mug and turned his stool around and leaned against the bar. His hawk-like eyes scanned the room and took a small draw of ale.

"I doubt they'll have much luck. They would be better served to freelance."

The barkeep nodded as he tore a chunk from an old loaf of bread and stuffed it in his mouth. "Yep, too bad too. Demetrin's whole crew were not rat-men. It would have taken an army to take down a guild like that."

Pavicious let those words sink in and a wry smile crept across his face. He whirled his chair around, sloshing some ale out on the counter as he did. "You still able to get a hold of Grascon?"

The barkeep frowned as he wiped up the spilled ale. "Yeah, he just got back from Nalir. Been working with that king down there for some pretty baubles."

"Tell him to meet me in the common room of the Blue

Dragon Inn tomorrow at midday." Pavicious said as he took another long draw from his mug. The fat thief slid the half empty flagon to the bar keep and hoped down from the bar.

"Pav-co, what do you expect me to say to make him show up?"

Pavicious smiled as he started out of the door. "Tell him

Demetrin gave me something that he might enjoy."

Pavicious made his way out into the streets and figured he better find a place to hold up for the night. The chubby thief caught movement out of the corner of his eye. He glanced over and across the street and up a block , he spied a dark form lifting an apple from a fruit vendor that was open way too late. The form's movements looked strangely familiar to him. He was amazed that he could not only see that far in the dark, but to see that far and so clearly. He started over toward the shadowy figure. If it was who he thought it was, his luck was improving by the second.

* * *

Kellacun wiped the tears from her eyes and tried to ignore the growing hunger in her belly. It seems the change takes a strong toll on her body and she was needing to eat. With her parents murdered and no money, she was going to have to resort to petty thievery to get by.

She made her way through an alley toward the rough spots in town. She knew the vendors often stayed open longer than normal because the guards patrolled there less often. The rogue spied a small grocer, selling fruits to drunks outside of a rough and tumble bar known as The Gut. Though being a woman alone in the night near The Gut was a foolish endeavor, she figured her new found abilities could scare off any would be attackers. Kellacun ducked low in the corner shadow and snatched a few apples from a basket. She felt bad for stealing and memorized the street vendor's location, so she could pay her back later. As much as she hated the Duke, she was not going to turn into her father, either. Kellacun ducked back into the alley and munched down the first apple very quickly. She had polished the second and started to eat it when she remembered her father's friend, Soranna.

Kellacun's ears detected a slight shuffle across the alley floor in front of her. She pretended not to hear it, but placed her hand near her dagger.

"Kellacun, is that you?" a familiar voice called out.

"Pavi?" Kellacun asked, not believing her ears! *Was there a friendly voice still alive? If he lived, did her father live as well?*

Pavicious stepped from the shadows. "It is you! By the stars, I thought you had been killed by the hunters!"

Kellacun rushed into his arms, almost dropping her half eaten apple. "Pavi, they killed mamma!" She said in a wail of tears.

He hugged her and stroked her face. "I know. They killed us all. Even killed me, but your father gave me the gift just before I was stabbed in the back by the elf bitch. I can't figure out why her swords worked on Demetrin and not me? I have the gift now too." he said in a rush.

Kellacun's nose twitched nervously. Pavicious smelled different but she could not put her finger on it. *Was it the gift?* Cleary he had not bathed in some time, but there was something else. Something feral about him. "So you have the gift? I mean you can transform?"

Pavicious nodded. "Yes, I think so. I have not done so yet, but wounds heal on me super quick, and despite my chubbiness, I don't get tired as fast. I can run and jump better than I ever have. I can hear and smell things others cannot. Not to mention, see in the dark. It is no wonder

Demetrin was able to fight against the Duke so easily!"

Kellacun sat back against a crate in the alley. "So how do you think you …turn it on?"

Pavicious shrugged his shoulders. "I remember Demetrin telling me it had something to do with the moon."

Kellacun nodded and pulled the last apple from her pouch and started eating. "So what now, Pav-co?"

He narrowed his eyes. "I am going to start the guild back up. I will make it bigger than your father ever had it. We will move to the sewers where the city guard don't dare to follow. I will be a king!"

Kellacun did not look up. "I am going to avenge the murder of my friends and family."

"You mean you are going to try to kill the elf and her hunters? You will die a fool!" Pavicious said with a chuckle.

"Why not kill the Duke himself why you are at it?" Kellacun narrowed her eyes, but did not respond.

"You're serious, aren't you? You do plan on killing all of them! I don't know whether to laugh or applaud your gusto.

You are just like your father."

Kellacun felt the rage burning up inside of her. "I am no thief, Pav-co!"

"Oh? I assume you paid for that apple that's in your hand?" Pavicious countered with a chuckle. "Don't be a fool, Kellacun. You are a beautiful young woman with no family. How will you survive?" Pavicious extended his hand. "Be my queen. We will rule the underworld and we will make Blackhawk work for us!"

Kellacun ignored his hand and started to walk down the alley. She took a final bite of her apple and tossed it into an empty alley crate. "Like the deal he made with my father?

Goodbye, Pav-co. Stay out of my way."

Pavicious growled. "How dare you? Where will you go?

How will you eat? You need me!"

Kellacun turned before exiting the alley. The wind blew her long black hair about her head. "Where will I go? Most likely to the abyss for the crimes I'm about to commit. It will be a fitting place for a monster like me."

Pavicious snarled and kicked the crates next to him. They tumbled over into a heap. He glanced around the alley and started back to the bar.

"I need a drink." he mumbled to himself.

* * *

Kellacun made her way through the dark winding alleys of Central City. She paused and knocked at an old rickety door that was affixed to a cellar that was under an old abandoned building. The structure had long since crumbled and only a large pile of rubble and debris remained. She waited for several moments before the gray cellar doors opened, revealing a frail old woman. She had long white hair and a dark creased face. She wore a thin white shawl over a gown and held a small candle to light the night.

"Kellacun, child. Do come in." The old woman said.

Kellacun smiled warmly. "How did you know it was me, Soranna?"

The old woman smiled and led Kellacun down a dark and crumbling stair case. "I remember you, though you have grown. How is your father? Is he fairing well against Ulsta?"

Kellacun felt her heart sink and she fought back tears. "He is passed, Soranna. They killed papa and momma last night."

Soranna paused on the dank passage and gave Kellacun a hug. "I am sorry, my dear. I told him that he should flee the city, that the Al-Kalidian was too much for him."

Kellacun did not answer. She buried her face into Soranna's shoulder and cried. She felt her chest heave and her belly tighten as she cried for everything. The loss of her parents, the loss of her way of life, and the loss of Joshua.

"Hush, child." Soranna broke the embrace. "Let's get you in and fill you with soup. You have the stink of a rat on you, and that means you're hungry."

Kellacun sniffed and wiped a lock of her black hair that had come matted on her cheek from her tears.

"What do you mean?"

Soranna held the candle up with her feeble arm and led them further down the passage. "All of our people have a smell to them. The newer ones stink the most. Fresh meat, if you will. A coppery smell, like blood. Yours is not like any I have smelled. When were you bitten?"

Kellacun frowned. "Bitten? I was never bitten. Bitten by what?"

Soranna paused at a larger, thicker reinforced door at the end of the passage. She handed Kellacun the candle and reached into her pocket for a set of tiny keys. "When did your father give you the gift? I smell it on you. As well as you smell it on me, but mine is much older," she said with a wry smile.

"I transformed for the first time tonight." Kellacun answered.

Soranna fumbled with the keys until she found a small brass one and inserted it into the heavy door. She turned it gently until a loud click echoed in the passage. The old frail woman nudged the door with her shoulder and the heavy portal creaked open. "So my question, child, is when were you bitten? You have to of received the gift somehow."

Kellacun ducked under the low door frame and into the room. It was completely black, save for the small candle that Soranna had placed on a thick oak table. The room was well furnished and completely round. The walls were made of thick stone and there was a wide ledge that spanned all the way around. Various pots and pans, along with baskets of food wares rested on the wide stone ledge.

Soranna gestured for Kellacun to sit and began to fumble with a tea pot. "Sit, my dear. I will make us some tea."

Kellacun glanced around the room, surprised that she could see so well in the darkness. She thought she smelled what Soranna was talking about. She had a dark musty smell that resembled a coppery blood like odor.

Soranna turned and walked back to the table. She placed a cup down in front of each of them and poured hot steaming tea from the metal pitcher. "There you go child, sit."

Kellacun frowned. "How did you heat that up? You have no furnace, or fire?"

Soranna waved her hand and smiled as she sipped her tea. The chair behind Kellacun rocketed forward and hit her in the back of the legs. Kellacun lost her balance and fell back into the chair as it scooted her forward to the table. "See, sitting is much more relaxing, isn't it, child?" Soranna slid a small dish that contained bright crystal cubes of sugar and a basket of fresh fruit to the befuddled rogue.

Kellacun glanced down at her chair before dismissing the woman's strange talents. Her father had told her that she was a witch. Kellacun smiled nervously and dropped two cubes of sugar into the tea and took a bite from one of the apples. The fruit was fresh and sweet. She could feel her stomach growl impatiently for her to eat more.

"So, tell me how you got the gift from your father?" Soranna asked.

Kellacun shrugged as she chewed. "I don't know. I changed for the first time last night."

Soranna narrowed her eyes and placed her tea down.

"But, when were you bitten?"

"I was never bitten. It just happened. Joshua told me my parents were to be arrested, I rushed in and saw momma laying on the floor in a pool of blood." Kellacun choked down her sobs. "A large man wearing a horned helm erupted from the darkness to kill me. Joshua started fighting it. It cut off his arm…" Kellacun trailed off into tears.

"Now now, you did the smart thing by running. A hunter is a monster that's powers are beyond you." Soranna said. "Drink more tea."

Kellacun wiped her tears and frowned. "Run? I didn't run. I couldn't abandon Joshua. When I saw it hurting him, I felt a terrible hate come out of me and I transformed.

Except, I didn't know I had."

"So you managed to distract the hunter to get Joshua out. Very noble." Soranna said.

Kellacun frowned as a disgusted look crept on her face. "My father didn't raise me to be a coward, Soranna. I killed the man with Joshua's dagger. I ran when the guards were coming. Not because I was afraid, but because of what I had

become. I didn't know what to do."

Soranna cast a raised eyebrow of doubt.

"So who is Joshua?"

"Joshua Blackhawk is my truest love."

Soranna choked on her tea. "The Duke's son? You are courting the Duke's son!?"

"Not really courting, he has a wily charm about him. We are to be married." Kellacun said with a warm reminiscent smile.

Soranna's face twitched and she shot up from her chair. "You listen to me, and you listen well. If the Duke finds out that you exist, let alone who you are, you will be killed. I don't entirely believe your story with the hunter, nor do I comprehend how you claim to be a wererat and have never been bitten. It doesn't work like that."

Kellacun felt the rage building in her, but she fought it back down. "I don't claim to be anything other than my father's daughter."

Soranna let her fear and anger subside. "Kellacun, child. Do you know the danger you are in? Have you ever heard of the Al-Kalidian?"

Kellacun sunk her shoulders. "I haven't. All I know is that I will find justice for my parents."

Soranna slid over and placed a comforting arm around

Kellacun. "Love, Ulsta Al-Kalidious is from the Al-Kalidian Vale. One of the most deadly military elven vales from the old times. She is as wicked as she is calculating. If you truly did kill one of her hunters, she will know you exist and will scour this city until she finds you. She has the aid of magic that has been brought down from millennia of old. Don't throw away your life. Flee this city."

Kellacun fought back the tears that began to well up in her tired blue eyes. "But what of Joshua? I can't abandon him."

"You must. If he were to go with you, the duke would hunt you both down. As would Ulsta." Soranna said sadly.

"Then I will kill them."

Soranna hugged her. "I understand why you would feel that way. But, is it worth it?"

Kellacun met the old gray eyes of Soranna with her bright fiery blue. "I will think of nothing other than their deaths, until I make it so."

"And then what, you silly girl? Are you and Joshua going to live happily ever after? Does your pretty little mind actually think that he will love you after you kill his father? He will most likely try to kill you. So be prepared for the day you must make the choice of your life or his." Kellacun shook her head.

"Our love is stronger than that."

"Is it? Then where is your love, Kellacun? Why is he not here?" Soranna got up and moved to an old chest.

Kellacun did not answer. Reality struck her like a heavy war maul. "If it comes to that, justice will guide my blade."

Soranna opened the chest and pulled out several linen sheets and a mesh hammock. "You can sleep in this. Tomorrow we will work on getting you that blade. If you are truly a natural wererat, you are a wolf among sheep here in Central City."

Kellacun nodded distantly. "So how do you know my father?"

Soranna looked over her shoulder and smiled as she set up the hammock. "Your father is from a small town south of here, called Bureland. He came to Central City as an apprentice in the Mason's Guild after his service in the orc wars."

"My father was in the orc wars?" Kellacun asked.

"Yes, he was fairly popular. He defeated the leader of a Kar during one of the battles and claimed the warrior's silver cutlass."

"I don't recall him ever having a sword like that." Kellacun said.

Soranna smiled. "I have it, dear. He didn't like to use it."

"So then what happened?" Kellacun asked as she munched down another apple and a hunk of bread.

"The top one hundred were contracted to build the coliseum. They worked for most of the first year and well into the second. When they were close to finishing, the Duke backed out of the agreed contract and tried to renegotiate with the guild leaders for a lesser sum."

"I don't know the exact amounts, but many of the apprentices were not going to be paid for several of the months that they had worked. Your father had been saving for a wedding for he and Mara, your mother. The guild leaders initially resisted the Duke, but one by one they started giving in."

"Though the vote was to accept the new contract, Demetrin got the men behind him and overthrew the guild. They tried to murder him, but failed. His service in the orc wars made him a formidable adversary and then after two of the eight guild leaders joined his ranks, they abandoned the guild. Almost two thirds of the Mason's Guild went with him, but the remaining thirty or so stayed."

"So what did they do?" Kellacun asked.

Soranna finished tying the hammock and shook out the linen sheets. "They noticed that this was a common practice for the Duke. That was how he controlled businesses and other financial venues that he didn't have any money invested in. So, Demetrin and the others started stealing and attacking his businesses."

"So what did the Duke do?" Kellacun asked with interest.

"He did what any man of villainy would do. He hired an assassin to come in and kill the group. Hired some wererat from Dawson. No one ever learned his name. After the killer had cut their numbers in half, Demetrin and Grascon set a trap for the fiend. Both were bit, but only your father contracted lycanthrope. Grascon left the guild and the city. Demetrin used his new found abilities and became more aggressive in his methods and tactics. Well, at least until recently. The Duke must have paid thousands of gold to get one of the Al-Kalidians to come in."

"So how does stealing from innocents help fight the Duke?" Kellacun asked angrily as she thought about her father leading the guild.

Soranna tossed a pillow down on the hammock and crooned an angry finger at Kellacun. "Watch your misguided judgments, child. Your father put the squeeze on illegal businesses that the duke operated. He closed down three of them last month. Why do you think the Duke hired the assassins?"

Kellacun smiled warmly to hear the truth of her father and not what she had guessed the last few hours. "I will kill them, Soranna. If my father was brave enough to stand against them, so am I."

Soranna smiled and gestured to the hammock. "Get some rest, girl. You are as foolish as you are brave. I guess the apple never falls far from the tree. Tomorrow, I will begin getting you some proper equipment if you are to survive against the Al-Kalidian. For now, toss out those ragged old clothes. Tomorrow, we will fix you up nice."

Kellacun slowly pulled off her clothes and tossed them to the floor. She climbed into the hammock and under the thin sheets. They felt smooth and cool against her bare skin. "Soranna," Kellacun called out.

The old woman turned as she blew out the candle and climbed into bed. "Yes, my child?"

Kellacun smiled warmly. "Thanks."

4
The Severed Heart

Pavicious cursed to himself as he made his way back to The Gut. Who does she think she is? A stupid fool girl, that's who. What makes her think she can take on the entire magistrate?

Even Demetrin couldn't do that.

He made his way to the rowdy bar and walked inside. The strong odor of booze and smoke wafted into him as the fat thief stormed his way to the bar.

"Back so soon?" the barkeeper asked.

Pavicious grumbled and tossed a few silver coins down on the bar as he roughly hopped up on the stool. "Just keep

'em coming."

The barkeep filled a wooden flagon and slid it over to him. A bit of the ale sloshed out and landed on the grumpy rogue's arm and made a small puddle in front of him. "I said give me a drink, not a bath, you louse." Pavicious growled.

"Louse?" the barkeep asked.

Pavicious slammed the empty flagon down on the counter. "Don't talk, just keep them coming."

The barkeep bit his bottom lip as he refilled the mug and slid it to Pavicious before casting a sidelong glance to the bouncer standing against the wall. He was about six foot tall and was well muscled. His face was scarred and his jagged ears housed several sets of shiny gold earrings. The man was not entirely human, and his square jaw and under bite marked him for having some orc in his ancestry, though it was difficult to pinpoint.

Pavicious slammed drink after drink as the night progressed under the watchful eye of the bouncer that stood with his arms folded. Patrons began to slowly filter out as Pavicious continued to drink. The fat rogue finished his mug and roughly set it down as his head wobbled low.

"One, more fer' da' road." he said with a thick tongue.

The barkeep shook his head from side to side. "We're closing. You need to take your drunk ass out of here."

"Fine." Pavicious said as he slid from the stool and onto wobbly legs. The bar seemed to shift and rotate in his stupor as he staggered to the door. He made his way to the door frame and leaned against it. The cool wood felt good against his hot head. "See you tomorrow," he stammered and wandered into the street.

"You can't take the mug of ale with you, fatty." The barkeeper snarled.

Pavicious did not answer and stumbled into the street with the wooden mug.

The barkeeper pointed to the bouncer "Go find that fat lard and teach him some respect. And then, bring back my mug."

The bouncer smiled and snatched up a large wooden cudgel from the side of the bar. It had a wide iron band around the end that was capped with round studs. The bouncer patted the club in his hands as he started out to follow Pavicious.

Pavicious staggered into the street. It was late at night and he silently cursed himself for drinking so much. Seeing Kellacun again roused some emotion from deep inside his loins, and he needed to forget the little minx. But now, he was in no state to make his way to an inn. He leaned against the cool brick wall of the bar and decided to sleep it off in the alley. It would not be the first time in his life he had done such, and he figured it would not be his last.

He stumbled and staggered into the alley and leaned back against some crates. "Sing with me, alley rats!" he called out. "There once was a man from Nantuckett" Pavicious continued to sing, holding his fat belly and belching between verses. "And he carried his coins in a bucket."

Pavicious lurched forward as he was shoved from behind. He landed hard on the stone alley floor and spilled his mug of ale. "You spilled my ale." he said in a whiny voice.

"You're gonna' pay, fatty," the bouncer taunted.

Pavicious sat up in the alley and held his mug upside down above his mouth, letting the last few drops fall into his gaping maw. "Poor ale. It's all gone."

Before Pavicious could turn to the bouncer, the heavy cudgel struck him in the side of the head. His limp form fell awkwardly to the alley floor. The bouncer kneeled down and picked up the mug. "Learn some respect, you fat tub of lard. Demetrin ain't here to protect yer' filthy ass no more."

The muscled man walked angrily back to the bar, leaving the unconscious Pavicious to the night.

* * *

"Did you see that?" Lucas said as he stopped foraging through the dead man's pockets.

"Aye. Grumble bounced him good!" Spot said with a chuckle. "Serves the fat bastard right."

Lucas slipped a few copper coins into his pouch and removed the dagger he had stuck in the poor man's back. He wiped his dirty blonde hair and stood up. He was well over a hand taller than Spot.

Spot rubbed the burn scars that covered the right side of his face. It had little feeling and he bitterly recalled the burns that Demetrin had given him. "Too bad that rat,

Demetrin, is dead. I owe him a lot of pain."

Lucas chuckled and stepped over the dead man they had robbed. Lucas was tall and thin, and his long bowl shaped haircut did not suit him well. "Want me to go stick my dirk in fatty too? Maybe we can make it look like they killed one another."

Spot nodded his head. "Yea, go stick the oaf. Might as well claim responsibility to finishing off the last of the rat-man's men. But don't bother trying to make it look like anything. Since fatty's broke, would have to leave our money in fatty's pockets to make it look like a robbery"

Lucas walked over and kneeled down next to Pavicious. "He ain't dead." he said. "Should we kill him? After all, we don't need the guard after us for any more trouble than we aim to stir."

"Who cares?" Spot said. "He's dead already, remember.

They dumped his body into the mass grave south of town.

Can't get in trouble for killing a dead man." Lucas shrugged and plunged his dirk deep into Pavicious's chest. He smiled as Pavicious unconscious form gurgled and lurched. He twisted the blade as best his skinny arms would allow, and then pulled out the knife and slid it in his belt. He rummaged through the fat thief's pockets and removed several coins, all the while he giggled as Pavicious gurgled on his own blood.

"Stop playing and let's go." Spot ordered through gritted teeth.

Lucas kicked Pavicious in the face and laughed as he hurried to catch up to Spot. "So much for the guild he was going to start."

* * *

Joshua wiped warm wet tears from his face as he stared off into the night. How did this happen? It was spinning out of control so rapidly. He couldn't let Kellacun throw her life away. Joshua hurried over to his chifferobe and began to get dressed. He slid on his thin chain shirt and strapped his bright brass colored greaves to his shins.

"Are you sure you should be going out tonight, Master Joshua?" Augusta asked.

Joshua looked up as he hurriedly tightened his sword belt. Augusta was dressed in his usual fine blue silk servant attire. Even for a servant, Augusta's elegant poise was never ending. "There is a killer on the loose, Augusta. I aim to stop her."

Augusta arched an eyebrow and neatly placed the folded towels down on Joshua's bed. "Master Joshua, your father's men are surely capable. There is no need for you to go out." Joshua stood and strapped a small brass colored shield to his arm. It was brilliantly shiny and was bare of a scar or scratch. He examined it before unstrapping and placing it on his back. He hooked a grappling hook under the stone ledge of his window. "You can inform against me if you wish, Augusta. But I am heading out tonight, either way."

Augusta smiled a creased grin and closed the door lightly. As soon as it latched he started down the crimson carpeted hall of the palace, Augusta mumbled to himself. "The killer you seek is not hidden in the streets, Master

Joshua. He is living comfortably well within this palace."

Joshua quickly climbed down the rope, despite his missing hand. He gave it a quick flip and the small grappling hook tumbled down and clanged in the alley. He glanced around the dark before coiling the rope around his elbow and then attached it to his belt. Without a word, he ducked into the darkness of the city.

* * *

Pavicious opened his eyes and squinted at the bright sun. He rolled over onto his belly and moaned, resting his aching head on the cool alley bricks. He still felt mildly intoxicated and his head felt as if a hundred warhorses had stomped on it. The chubby thief struggled to his feet and pondered the strange tear in his shirt and the dried blood stains. There were some on his collar and a larger spot near the tear in his chest. Pavicious recalled his arranged meeting with Grascon and his mind quickly abandoned the blood as he stumbled out into the street.

Pavicious hurried through the busy Central City streets and rushed into the Blue Dragon Inn. The common room was bare save for the huge bleached white skull of some sort of serpent that the owner claimed was the skull of a blue dragon. The barkeeper was no where to be found, but his large bouncer was standing at the corner of the bar, eying Pavicious suspiciously. The man was clearly a half-orc. The chubby thief knew him immediately by repute as Glaszric. He was one of the few half-orcs that dared to live in Central City since the orc wars. Glaszric's skin had an obvious green hue and his thick jaw and under bite marked him as a halforc without question.

Pavicious waded through the tables and chairs and took a seat at the far end of the room, near a large wooden stage that often held dancing girls or, depending on the night, a covey of bards. After wiping his sweaty grimy brow with his dirty sleeve, Pavicious waved at the serving wench.

The serving wench looked down on the dirty fat thief. "Ale?"

Pavicious looked her up and down. She was attractive and he even smelled a hint of perfume. "How about lunch with you?"

"Ale and lunch for just you, it is." She answered and walked away.

Pavicious chuckled at her response and smiled as he watched her go. As soon as he built this guild he was going to build himself a large harem. The fat thief pondered his future when he spied Grascon as he entered the common room. He was a small man with dark brown hair that dangled about his face when he walked. He moved with a swagger that bordered on cocky. The rogue wore a thin rapier at his side and his dirty brown clothing was covered with a black cloak.

Grascon moved to the table and sat down. He was unshaven and smelled of filth and sewer. "What do you want, fatty? Make it quick."

Pavicious smiled as the waitress handed him his ale, and then turned back to Grascon. "It's simple," he said as he took a drink. "I have Demetrin's gift and I look to start a guild."

Grascon pulled a small silver flask from a leather pouch on his belt and took a swig. He grimaced briefly and smiled as he replaced the cork. "Got the gift, do ya? Well it did

Demetrin a lot of good, didn't it?"

Pavicious smiled as the serving wench set him a plate of fish and several slices of bread before turning back to Grascon. "Yea, but I see it differently than that fool." "How so?"

Pavicious stuffed a bite of fish into mouth. "I look to infect every one of my guild members."

Grascon took another swig from his flask and rubbed his scraggly chin. "So you just expect to dole the gift out like a cheap whore?"

Pavicious stuffed his mouth and took a long draw from his flagon. "No. The loyal thieves who have proved themselves will earn the gift. After they earn a certain amount of coin, they will be rewarded. One could say, I am going to sell it."

Grascon narrowed his eyes. "And what is to stop your new recruits from infecting their own little guild and running you out of business?"

Pavicious smiled and tossed a small bag on the table. "You."

Grascon eyed the coins suspiciously before leaning forward on the table. "Unless that is full of silver, you can't afford me, fatty."

"Work with me, and in a few months that will be full of gold." Pavicious said, stuffing another bite of fish and bread into his mouth.

Grascon popped the cork of his flask and took another swig. "So, assuming that I want to join this guild of yours, where will you stage so that devil elf bitch won't hunt us down like Demetrin's boys?"

Pavicious smiled as he chewed his oversized bite. "The sewers, of course." He waved his fork in the air. "It will take some time to find a good location, but while I am recruiting, our new members can begin building the safe house." "First, we will need to knock off Spot and his crew.

They'll be a thorn in our side if we don't." Grascon said. "They were bragging about killing you last night… Bragged they cut your heart in half."

Pavicious smiled and glanced down at his shirt. "Well that explains the tear and the bloodstains."

"So what are you going to call this new guild?" Grascon glanced about the room to notice it was filling up with the lunch crowd.

Pavicious chewed his lip and pondered for a moment. "How about The Severed Heart Guild? Since Spot tried to cut mine in half."

Grascon snatched a drink from the serving wench's tray as she walked by. "It does have a certain jingle to it."

* * *

Kellacun opened her tired eyes and the dark world came into view. She placed her face into her down pillow as she fought away her sleepiness. It had been a long night and she was plagued with dreams of her mother's body and the fight with the hunter. She laid face down for several minutes before forcing herself upright. Kellacun moaned a little and kept the smooth silk sheets against her breasts. She wished her parents would have had sheets like these. They were so soft. She silently cursed herself. If she were wishing, why not wish them alive again.

Kellacun rubbed her weary eyes in the dimly lit room and lazily slid her feet off of the hammock. The cold stone floor made her wish for her slippers. She scanned the room lazily as she tried to wake up and saw an unusual outfit hanging on the chair next to her. It was a smooth black silk garment that had hard leather patches of armor sewn into it. She stood up from her bed and ignored the cold stone floor. The tug from the bed sheets held her fast and she soon dropped them. She placed her arms over her cold breasts and lightly stepped to the chair. Alongside the black and red silk outfit was a bright shining silver cutlass. It was lighter and thinner than a normal cutlass, but was much larger than the rapiers that her father's men used. Used to use. She thought to herself.

Kellacun reached down and felt the silk apparel. To her surprise it was hard like leather, but was as flexible as silk. It was like nothing she had ever felt before. She rubbed her cold arms and held the outfit up before her. It was similar to her previous one, but it was obviously made for battle.

Kellacun jumped as the door to the room burst open.

She scrambled to cover her nakedness and held the outfit against her skin. It felt warm and smooth to the touch, almost as if it were alive.

"Put that on, child" Soranna said as she casually walked across the room with a sack of groceries. "See how it fits."

Kellacun awkwardly held the garment against her body.

"What is it?"

Soranna continued putting the tubers and a loaf of bread into her cabinets. "It's an outfit your father had prepared for

you since you were very young."

"My father?" Kellacun asked skeptically.

"Just put the damn thing on, child."

Kellacun sheepishly tried to slip the item on without exposing her nakedness.

"For heaven's sake, Child. Just put it on. I have seen a naked woman before. But I must admit, one built like you is more suited for street work than a warrior,." Sorrana said with a chuckle.

Kellacun fumed and her anger absolved her shyness. "Oh, I will work the streets, old woman. You can count on that."

Soranna smiled and pulled two wooden bowls from the cabinet and dumped some oats in each. "You are a feisty one, girl. I reckon your father knew what he was doing when he was teaching you."

Kellacun slid her legs into the garment and then placed her arms in. "How does it fasten in the back?"

"It will fasten on its own."

Kellacun frowned. "How will it do that?"

Soranna did not answer and poured some water into a copper pan and placed it over the fire. Kellacun was startled when the garment's back suddenly came together behind her. She tried to look over her shoulder to see how it has fastened, but she could not see any clasps.

"Soranna, it fastened!"

"I know child. I told you it would."

Kellacun looked over the other shoulder astonished. "But how?"

"It's called demon skin. Your father paid a pretty penny to have it crafted for you."

"It's really the skin of a demon?" Kellacun asked somewhat disgusted.

Soranna smiled and channeled a basic flow of evocation and created a fire under the copper pan filled with water. "Kind of. It's hard to explain, child. And unless you plan on staying in the cellar with me for a few decades to understand the arcane arts, just take it for what it is."

Kellacun marveled for a bit longer before sliding her legs into the long knee boots. The combination of black and red reminded her of her father's Mason's Guild charter. They had chosen a spider to represent their talents, playing on the premise that a spider web was a perfect construction.

Soranna smiled as the water began to boil and poured the oats in. She stirred the pan softly as she gradually added more oats.

Kellacun strapped the sword to her hip. Its size betrayed its weight. She expected the blade to be much heavier than it was. It felt lighter than a rapier, let alone a sword that was nearly twice its density. She ran her gloved finger along the polished chrome hilt. It felt as smooth as glass to the touch.

"This sword is beautiful."

"As beautiful as a thing of wickedness can be."

Kellacun slouched and bit her lip. "Come on, Soranna. You have to admit, this sword is a piece of art as much as it is a tool for war."

Soranna looked up from her oats and gave the sword a half glace. "If you say so, child."

Soranna finished pouring all the oats in the pan. "As soon as we are done with breakfast, we have a lot of training to do."

Kellacun sat down at the table as Soranna placed a wooden bowl in front of her and she set one down for herself.

"What training?" Kellacun asked.

Soranna scooped heaping mounds of warm toasted oats in Kellacun's bowl and then filled her own. "Just a few lessons."

Kellacun smelled the oats. The warm aroma made her belly grumble. "So where did you get these things?" Soranna filled a pitcher with milk and set it on the table.

"Always with questions, child. But, never with answers."

Kellacun quickly poured the milk into her oats and cooled them off a bit. "Well, how am I to have answers, when I am just learning the questions?"

Soranna's old face wrinkled warmly with a smile as she scooped sugar into her oats. "That, child, is something a

young woman must learn."

"Come on, Soranna. Tell me."

The old woman pursed her wrinkled lips and blew on a heaping scoop of oats before answering. "The outfit your father had tailored for you. It will fit whoever puts it on. It

won't fit a halfling and wouldn't fit an ogre, but it fits any human sized person. Man or woman."

Kellacun sipped the oats and jerked her head when it burned her lips. She wiped her mouth and glanced down at the sword. "Okay, but what of the sword. Must I be a master in the arcane arts to understand it?"

Soranna finished blowing and ate the heaping bite. She chewed slowly and swallowed. "The sword is enchanted as well. Your father claimed it from an orc in the orc wars."

"An orc?" Kellacun asked in disbelief. The blade was much too masterful to be created by an orc. "There is no way an orc made this."

"Of course not, the sword was owned by a Darayal Legionnaire. One of the Sky Captains of old."

"A Sky Captain?" Kellacun asked excitedly. "You mean, like the ones far to the south? In the warm waters of Aboe and Ladathon?"

Soranna blew on another spoonful of oats. "Yes. The orc had used the enchanted blade to dozens of victories. Your father slew him and claimed the sword as his own."

Kellacun narrowed her eyes with doubt. "Wait a minute. If my father owned this sword, and it's so great, why didn't he use it against the Duke? Or against the elf assassins?"

"The same reason you will only want to use it sparingly.

Even with your gloves as protection, it will burn your skin."

Kellacun looked at the sword nervously. "Why would it burn me?"

Soranna chuckled as she took another big bite of oats.

"Because it's made of silver."

Kellacun relaxed a bit and took the sword in. The levity of the blade seemed to finally sink into her. She stood from the table and drew the sword. Its shiny polished silver blade seemed to amplify the light in the dimly lit cellar dwelling. She turned the blade over in her outstretched hand and measured its weight. It felt lighter than one of wood. "My father trained me with larger and heavier blades than the ones he used. He trained me since I was very young. Was it for this day?"

Soranna's smile slowly slipped away as she stirred her oats. "Child, I have listened to you rant last night. I want you to know that your father was a good man. Do not blame your mother's death on him. There is one man responsible for that."

Kellacun bit her bottom lip as she held the sword out in front her. She felt powerful for the first time in her life. "I understand, Soranna. My heart has been cut in two, but trust me when I say that I will make that man pay."

5
Lostos

"Check and make sure that there aren't any guards coming," Pavicious said as he gripped the heavy wooden grate with his chubby hands.

"Nope, we're clear. Doubt any guards would come this way anyway. They never patrol in The Gut."

"Good," Pavicious said as he wrenched up the heavy wooden sewer grate. Small black bugs and spiders scampered for cover from the morning light.

Grascon glanced down the exposed shaft. It was made of moss covered bricks and extended down into darkness.

"You sure this is a good idea?"

"Of course."

"Lots of unnatural predators make their home down here." Grascon said nervously. "I can fence with the best of sword fighters, but fighting beasts is much different."

Pavicious waved his hand in dismissal and lowered himself onto the iron ladder rung that was built into the stone wall. "No worries. Just like swordsmen, if you stick them, they will die."

Grascon watched Pavicious climb down the narrow ladder with an unnatural ease for a portly man. "You been here before, Pavy?

Pavicious stopped climbing and looked up. He paused briefly and climbed back up and stuck his head

from the shaft. "Another thing, no talking down here.
The sounds will echo and attract predators. We must be
extremely quiet. I learned some hand signals from
prison. We can use those and elaborate on them as our
guild grows."

Pavicious gave Grascon a quick run down before
starting back into the dark dank depths of the Central
City sewers. When he reached the bottom, he was
amazed at how well he could see in the dark sewer
corridors. And despite his heightened sense of smell,
the putrid odor of decay and feces did not seem to
assail him like it would have in the past.

Grascon climbed down from the ladder and covered
his nose with his cloak. The odor was difficult to bear
and it made his eyes water.

"Stinks," he signed.

Pavicious smiled and motioned for Grascon to
follow. The pair made their way down the wide sewer
corridor. It had large curved ceilings and the walls were
rounded as well, making the corridor a cast bricked
tube. In the center was a mid-sized stream of stagnant
water. Dead rat carcass and other debris floated in the
foul waterway.

Grascon tried his best to move silently but the
occasional pauses and glares from Pavicious told him
he was not doing as good of a job as he liked. The pair
moved deep into the sewers. The farther they went the
older the passages became. Large roots jutted out from
missing bricks and an occasional collapse side wall
made maneuvering through the infected water
necessary.

Pavicious would pause ever so often and then when Grascon would ask him what he was stopping for, the portly rogue would reply that he heard something getting eaten and to keep moving.

"Whatever you're looking for, it's clearly not here." Grascon whispered as loud as he dared.

Pavicious stopped and rubbed his chin. "I remember it was around here someplace. Dee took me here once… Said he found it in his travels."

Grascon rubbed his nose and wiped the tears from his eyes. "I think we should head back. There are dozens of cellars that we can use. If we move often, it is unlikely the
Duke will find us."

Pavicious gave Grascon an angry glare. "Are you kidding me? He rooted us out quite easily before. We will find this place. If you can't hack it, go back up."

Grascon narrowed his eyes. "I'm not some street cut purse novice, fat ass. If you want to insult me, then do it. We can draw steel here and see who is the better man."

Pavicious chuckled to himself and stepped over the skeletal remains of a man, "Stow it. Put your ego away and help me look. It's around here somewhere."

Grascon stood ready on the narrow ledge that surrounded the edges of the sewer corridors.

"There it is!" Pav-co exclaimed louder than he wanted. He rushed over to the wall on the other side of the sewer, ignoring the filthy water as he waded through.

Grascon relaxed a bit. "I don't see anything."

"It's right here. On this wall. We need to find a brick that triggers the door."

Grascon navigated his way across the putrid water as best he could without immersing himself into it. Once on the other side, he kicked muck from his boots and made his way to Pavicious. "Are you sure this is it?"

Pavicious nodded with a big smile. "Yep. I remember this wall well."

"What do you mean, you remember it well? I thought you were only here once."

"I was. I mean, this wall just jumps out at me. Maybe it is the brick pattern. I don't know. I just know this is it."

Grascon stared at the wall for a moment and then looked at the surrounding walls. "Pavie, it looks the same as the others."

"Not to me." Pavicious ran his fingers over the mossy stones. "Here!" He pushed a brick. The stone moved inwards ever so slightly and the wall made a grumbling sound. Gears and mechanisms clattered quietly from the other side and the wall opened slightly. "See."

Grascon looked at the whole event with astonishment before following Pav-co inside. "You think there are any of those giant grub worms in there?"

Pavicious stepped through the portal. "Nah."

"What makes you so sure?"

"If there had been, they would have heard you and attacked by now."

Grascon quieted down and nervously looked into every shadow.

The pair made their way down the narrow corridor. The floors and walls were covered in a mossy brick, but it was less damp than the sewers. They continued on a few hundred feet and came to a large wooden door. The outside bore the shape of a floating head. It had a mouth that was agape with hundreds of sharp pointed teeth. There was a single eye above the mouth and the top of the head had dozens of small stalks that each bore an eye on the end of it.

"A beholder." Grascon mumbled.

"A what?"

Grascon moved closer to the carving. "A beholder. It's a mythical monster of untold power. It's the symbol of many cults and sects. The monster represents safety and protection. Powerful demons and denizens of the dark are rumored to have summoned these beasts to guard their treasures."

Pav-co ran his hand across the beholder. It was made of wood, like the door, but neither showed any signs of aging. "It must be enchanted, or it would show signs of rotting from the damp air."

Grascon shook his head and backed away. "We need to leave, Pavicious. Enchanted doors with beholder carvings…

This isn't a place for us."

Pav-co chuckled and waved his hand in dismissal. "Don't be a fool. Dee used to come here all the time. If there was some evil cult, he would have said so. Now, help me find the opening mechanism."

Grascon stood back nervously. "Seriously, Pav-co. I think we need to leave."

Pav-co ignored him and continued to twist and pull on the door.

Grascon watched for a few seconds. "Try the mouth."

Pav-co turned. "Seriously?"

Grascon nodded. "Yeah, I heard the cults often placed the mechanisms in the mouth."

Pav-co peered into the mouth area. There was a slight recess and a lever near the tongue. He reached inside and gently pushed on the lever. He smiled as he heard a click.

"That ought to do it."

Grascon nervously pulled on the bottom teeth and the large heavy door glided open.

Pavicious slid through. "Mind your blade, Grascon. I think we have some current residents."

Grascon slid through the door. There was a long hallway with stairs ascending up on either side. The right and left walls each had a top balcony with thick pillars extending up to the tall ceiling. There were four sconces on the walls that were aflame. "A sconce will stay lit for about twenty four hours before it needs more oil."

Grascon nodded. "That means we have company. I told you we should have left. Now, we are going to have to fight some cult."

Pavicious stepped towards the sconce and sniffed. "Wait a minute. There's no smell of pitch or oil in the air."

Grascon frowned. "You can smell that?"

Pav-co cautiously stepped to the sconce. He waved his hand over it. "No heat."

"What?"

"No heat. It's magical."

Grascon trotted over to Pav-co. He moved his hand over the sconce. "You're right."

Pavicious checked each sconce. "They're all magical. No one is here, they are always lit."

Grascon relaxed. "What's in the other chambers? The place could use a little fixing up, but all and all, it's like a palace."

"I think we have found our new guild hall."

Grascon nodded and opened the door to another elaborate chamber. "This is an amazing palace. It will work well."

Pav-co rubbed his chin. "I wonder why Dee didn't live down here all the time?"

Grascon glanced off at the door they had come through. "Some monsters do not embrace their wickedness. They desire to be what they once were."

"Oh, I'll be a monster," Pav-co growled. "One like they have never seen."

* * *

Kellacun sat in a wooden chair and tightly wound rope around her arm. The thin metal grappling hook was nestled between her thighs as she focused on her task.

Soranna looked up from her knitting. "You going out tonight, child?"

"Yes, I need to make sure the duke knows that all of the guild members are not dead."

"But, who is left child?"

Kellacun fastened the rope to her belt. "Me."

Soranna chuckled. "And how will that help you kill him? He will know of you soon enough."

Kellacun walked to the old woman. Her sleek black boots shined in the cellar's pale light. Kellacun leaned over and kissed the old woman on her forehead. "Not for him.

For the elf. I need her and her hunters to patrol again."

Kellacun paused before leaving the cellar. "I will be ok, Soranna."

"Just be careful, Kellacun. You know what happens to the hunter who looks for wolves."

Kellacun frowned. "What?"

"He finds them."

"I liken them more to a bee. I know I will be stung a few times, but I will crush it afterwards."

Soranna nodded. "Just be mindful, child. There is never just one bee."

Kellacun smiled as best as she could and closed the door. The old woman's words were not lost on her. She was going out to face a foe that had hundreds of years to train and another that had legions of men to protect him. How could she stand against them? She had to try.

Kellacun walked from the cellar stairs and stepped into the cool night air. The city was ending its long busy day. Merchants would be packing up and street urchins would be heading indoors. The drunkards and rats would soon be coming out. As Kellacun strolled through the dark alley, she chuckled at the difference between day and night. Central City went from a bustling metropolis to a dark and sinister place, riddled with shadows and the monsters that lived there.

She walked for several minutes before turning south toward her old home and the small market she often shopped at as a youth. The familiar walk pained her heart and she fought a tear. The young rogue knew she could never go home again.

"Hurry up!" Came a shout from around the corner.

Kellacun ducked low and peered around the edge of the alley wall. The inner market was nearly closed down and one of the Duke's tax wagons was there collecting from the poor. The wagon driver was shouting at the three other soldiers. They were all wearing Central City militia garb. The other soldiers were sitting in the rear of the wagon and shouting commands. There were two large heavy chests that Kellacun suspected were filled with the weekly tax collections throughout the city.

Kellacun inched closer in the darkening alley as the soldiers crossed off names on a scroll. It was surely a manifest to track the taxes paid. She watched with earnest as the soldiers tossed in the last bit of taxes into the chests. She could see the chest was littered with copper and steel coins. She even thought she saw a few wooden tokens. Wood tokens were used amongst the poor as currency for themselves. Her father had instituted that for them.

The wagon finished up and rode out from the market. Kellacun knew she had to get to it before it hit the main street. There was a larger secondary market just south of here and that would be her only chance.

She silently pushed off of the wall and sprinted through the dark alleys. Her keen vision and heightened dexterity allowed Kellacun to maneuver easily through the cluttered city corridor. Kellacun leapt to a stack of wooden crates and then to a sewer spout. Her powerful legs flexed and she leapt again to the building rooftop. The bright moon shined through the clouds as she darted across the rooftop and leapt to another gutter spout. Again she leapt, easily reaching the taller building's peak. It was a flat roof that over looked the larger market. It was a fitting place to confront the tax wagon.

Kellacun moved to the edge of the roof and loosed her grappling hook. She pulled a small metal loop and a hammer from her pack. She pounded the ring into the mortar, just under the lip of the roof. She hastily slid the rope through the loop and tied the end to the grappling hook. The rogue glanced down at the street and saw the tax wagon riding toward her. She knew she didn't have much time. She hastily slid the rope around her waste and fed it through several metal clips and a harness that she had seen her father use. She knew she could slow her decent with the rings by feeding the rope through them at several angles, relieving her own weight.

Kellacun finished and stood at the edge of the roof. The bright moon silhouetted her from behind as she gazed down at the unsuspecting tax wagon. She took a final breath to calm herself and then she stepped from the ledge. The rushing of the wind and the feeling of weightlessness shot rivers of excitement through her body. She ran down the wall towards the edge, giving herself slack on the rope for a near free fall. When she reached the edge of the wall, she tightened the slack and jumped out. The taught rope jerked her wide and the jump brought her out in a circle. Once she cleared the wall, she loosed the slack again as she hurled herself at the wagon from behind. She sailed through the air like a diving eagle she had heard stories about from the sailors.

The wagon came to her so fast, Kellacun did not have time to slow her approach. She kicked out and hit one of the tax men in the chest. She felt his ribs shatter from the blow as his body was hurled to the cobblestone street. Kellacun stood clumsily and drew her sword. She had not considered how to loose the scaling rope and her leg was numb from the collision.

"Bandits!" One of the guards shouted as they all drew their swords.

Kellacun parried a clumsy strike and lashed in with her cutlass. The keen weapon stabbed into the guard's shoulder. He cried out and fell from back of the cart. Kellacun ducked a slash from the third guard and turned to face him as the driver drew a spear from behind her.

He stabbed in. Kellacun swatted the blade down with the back side of her palm and slashed sideways, cutting the guard's sword arm. "Your days of stealing from the poor are at an end!"

The guard grabbed his arm in pain and jumped from the wagon. Kellacun started to turn when she felt a sharp pain in her back. The tip of a spear erupted from her belly. She felt her legs go numb and she struggled to stand.

"Die, bitch!" The guard growled.

Kellacun felt the transformation begin. She did not fight it and let it fall over her. She reached down with her clawed hands and snapped the tip of the spear off. She tossed it to the wagon bed and turned to face the driver. He backed away in fear and astonishment. The wound would have felled anyone, but still, the beast of a woman stood before him.

Kellacun pulled the shaft from her back and tossed it aside as she pointed her sword at the driver.

"Please, don't kill me. I have a family." The driver pleaded.

Kellacun recalled finding her mother dead on the floor of her home. How she had been beaten before her death. She recalled her friend Pavicious lying on the floor, dead as well. "A family?"

"Yes, I have a wife and a child."

Kellacun grimaced wickedly in her wererat form. "Good. They will understand how I feel when they mourn your death."

The driver put his hands up defensively as Kellacun brought her sword across. The keen blade severed the driver's head. His body crumpled to the floorboards of the wagon. The horses shuddered nervously, but the wagon break held them from a full panic.

Kellacun grabbed her belly as blood poured from the wound. She felt weak and cold. She kicked opened the chests and dumped the coins out in the street as she allowed herself to change back to her natural form. She thought the wound felt better in this way, but she still was aware that she may pass out. "Come, good people. Come to reclaim the tax money that has been stolen from you."

As the people began to poke their heads out from their homes and from the shadows they felt safe in, Kellacun hoisted the severed head above the chest. She let the blood drain for several seconds as she held it aloft. "This money was stolen from you by your murdering Duke. I am returning it in the name of justice. Leave it in the street, or take it home. It's yours to decide."

The citizens began to clamor out. They warily scooped up coins from the pile and filled their pockets. Some smiled, but all were nervous when standing before the bloodied rogue. Kellacun tossed the head into the chest and leapt down to the wounded guard. He was injured too severely to flee. "Can you drive the wagon?"

The guard spat at Kellacun's boots. She frowned and kicked the driver in the face. He groaned and lay on his back.

"I need someone to take a message to the Duke. If you're incapable of doing this, I can simply kill you and find another."

The guard turned his head to the side and spit blood onto the cobblestone street. "I can do it."

Kellacun reached down and easily tossed the man into the wagon. He landed roughly and let out another groan. Kellacun was amazed at her strength, but she did not let her emotions betray her surprise. She leapt in the back of the wagon as the guard struggled to get to his feet.

"Do you see this?" Kellacun held open the chest revealing the severed head of the wagon driver.

The guard narrowed his eyes and nodded.

"Tell the Duke that all he will ever harvest from the good people of this city is death. Death of his men, and if he

doesn't step down, death of himself." The guard didn't answer.

"Tell him, or I find another messenger."

"Okay." The guard said. The guard climbed in the driver seat and released the break.

Kellacun hopped down from the wagon and swatted the horse on the rump. "Tell him to send his elf bitch to me, so I can kill her for her crimes."

The guard smiled weakly as he rode off. "Oh, you can be assured he'll do that."

Kellacun smirked as the wound in her belly was already nearly healed. "That's what I am counting on."

* * *

"Where are we going?" Pavicious asked as he struggled to keep up with Grascon through the narrow city alleys.

"Now that we have a good location for the guild, I know two that we must recruit."

"Is there a reason we can't do it another time?"

Grascon jogged on. "Yea, but Spot is trying to recruit them as well. I think we should get to them first."

"So who are they?" Pav-co asked through labored breaths.

Grascon stopped at an alley intersection. "I think we are getting close. Time to be stealthy."

Pavicious smiled. "Now, that I can do. But, what are their names?"

"Kaisha and Ryshander."

"So who are they?"

Grascon motioned for quiet as he pointed around the corner. Pavicious peered around, using his ability to see in the dark to his advantage. He could see Spot and several of his friends. They were rested against the walls, or were seated recklessly against alley crates. A man and a woman walked up. The man was wearing a thin chain shirt that hung loosely under a tabard and he had a rapier at his hip. He had a small yellow sun emblem on his left shoulder that poked put from under his green cloak. The woman was about as tall as the man. She had long brown hair and was wearing leather armor. She was well endowed and Pav-co fantasized about what she would look like naked.

"Shit, we're too late." Grascon muttered silently.

Pavicious shifted his head. "I would like to plug my fat one into the girl. She is some piece of work."

Grascon shook his head. "Likely she would plug her sword into you, fatty. They were pirates on the pirate ship,

Undaunted."

Pavicious's eyes lit up. "The Aboe ship? The one that had dealings or run-ins with the monster minotaur that Dee always talked about?"

Grascon nodded. "That's the one."

"Sure would be nice to recruit them."

"Yea, but it looks like Spot beat us to it. It'll be hard to get them away, once Spot gets his hooks into them."

"Shouldn't be too hard." Pavicious countered.

Grascon waved his hand. "You think your wererat curse can solve everything. Well, it can't."

Pavicious motioned for Grascon to be quiet. "Shhh, I am trying to hear."

* * *

"You're late." Spot said arrogantly as he leaned against the wall. The other rogues chuckled or spit at the ground condescendingly.

Kashia shrugged. "I'd say we got here just when we wanted to arrive."

Spot pushed off of the wall and walked towards the pair. "Word on the street says you been cutting purses without my approval."

Ryshander stepped in front of Kaisha and moved his cloak back, revealing his sword. "There is no guild here, Spot. We can work as we want."

Spot glanced down at Ryshander's sword. "Pull your blade, fool. You will be dead in seconds."

Kaisha smiled disarmingly. "There is no need for bloodshed, Spot. No guild has marked the alleys."

"That's because I own the streets!" Spot snarled. "Now pay me ten gold crowns for your thievery and I will let you live."

Kaisha laughed. "Ten crowns!? We didn't make a tenth of that!"

Spot motioned to the other rogues before turning back to Kaisha. "Well then, death it is."

* * *

"What are they saying?" Grascon asked. He could tell by Ryshander's body language that the talks were going poor.

Pav-co half turned his head to keep an eye on the scene unfolding before him. "Spot wants gold for their recent activities and says he owns the streets."

Grascon chuckled. "Spot better be careful. I've seen them fight. Kaisha is as competent with a blade as Ryshander, though her fighting style suggests she did not serve on the Undaunted."

Pav-co waved his hand. "Who cares where she learned to fight? If she can stick a sword through our enemies then she is right with me."

Grascon pointed back to the group. "Looks like you will get a chance to see her skills."

Pav-co glanced back to the alley and watched Spot and his men draw their swords. "I think this is our chance to earn some favor."

6
A Villain is Born

Spot's men rushed in. Kashia hurled a small dagger from under her cloak. The small thin blade stuck in the thigh of one of the attackers. Ryshander quickly drew his rapier and parried a strike from one of the taller rogues.

"Back to back!" he shouted.

Kaisha drew her sword and moved to Ryshander's back. The wounded thief pulled the dagger from his leg and threw it back at Kashia. She easily avoided the poor throw as they stood in defense.

Pavicious stepped into the shadows of the alley. He was interested in recruiting the pair, but he wanted to kill Spot more.

"Help!" Ryshander called out, alerting Kaisha of a stabbing attack. She turned her body sideways allowing Ryshander to side step the strike instead of parrying it. With the attacker off-balance, Ryshander ducked low and stabbed in. His thin sword flexed as he gashed the rogue through the chest. The dying man gasped and fell to the ground.

Grascon paused at the edge of the alley. "Be careful, Pavie. I'm not getting myself skewered for those two."

Pavicious stalked forward, ignoring Grascon. He flexed his fingers as he moved behind Spot. The rogue leader stood with his arms folded under his chest as his men fought. The fat rogue quickly grabbed Spot around the neck and placed his knife tight against his throat. Spot froze in fear and did not move.

"You remember me, Spot?"

Spot's eyes went wide as he no longer focused on the scene before him. "Pavicious?"

"Yep. You should have made sure I was dead."

Spot stammered. "W-what are you talking about?"

Pavicious rammed the dagger deep into the side of Spot's neck. Hot coppery blood erupted from the wound and sprayed onto the dirt covered alley floor. "I won't make the same mistake."

"Spot's down!" One of the rogues called out as another rushed Pavicious.

Kaisha ducked a strike and parried another. "It seems we have help, my love."

Ryshander grunted in response as he continued to fight the street thugs. One of his attackers charged Pavicious. The fat rogue did not move. He merely placed his hands on his hips and smiled wickedly. The street thug rushed in and stabbed Pavicious through the chest. The portly wererat winced in pain and bit his lip, but did not falter. He paused briefly before starting his transformation into his wererat form.

The rogue released the blade in shock. "What are you?"

"I'm your killer." Pavicious stabbed the thin blade into the astonished rogue.

Ryshander and Kaisha slowed their defense as their attackers fled in fear.

Ryshander stepped between Kaisha and Pavicious. "We have no quarrel with you, monster."

Kaisha leaned close to Ryshander's ear. "Perhaps insulting the man is not the best approach to guarantee a peaceful resolution."

Ryshander smirked and continued to back away, keeping Kashia behind him.

Pavicious smiled. "You have nothing to fear from me,

Ryshander."

The thin pirate kept his blade pointed in defense. "Oh, I would not say. Your appearance seems to give me enough reason to be cautious."

Pav-co winced as he pulled the dagger from his chest. He exhaled slowly and examined the blade before tossing it to the ground. "My name is Pavicious. My friends call me

Pavie. I am the last survivor of our old guild."

Kaisha smiled. "We thank you for the rescue, Pavicious." "Pavie" he corrected.

"Yes, *Pavie*. But, it seems the city is not under an existing guild. My lover and I were just discussing that with Spot."

Pav-co let his body relax and he transformed back into a man. He checked the wound on his chest to make sure it was healing. He still was not quite used to being able to heal so rapidly. "Yes, I noticed." Pavicious gestured to the dead.

"I want to offer you a proposition."

Ryshander stepped forward. "What makes you different than the other wolves parading in the alleys?"

Kaisha placed her soft hand on Ryshander's shoulder. "Surely Pavie has earned a chance to explain his proposition, my love. Whether we needed it or not, he did bleed his tunic red to assist us."

Ryshander exhaled slowly. "You may have a few words, Pavicious."

Pav-co smiled and looked back to where Grascon had been. He did not see the assassin. He must be hunting down the stragglers he thought to himself. "I am starting a new guild. More powerful than the one before and greater rewards."

Ryshander spat on the ground. "I have never been in a guild. I worked on a ship once and I detest structured hierarchy."

Pavicious chuckled. "Me too. Think of this as more of a collection of friends. Work at your own pace. Make as much or as little as you want. All you must do is tithe the guild for maintaining the areas you work."

"And what if Kaisha and I do not want to join your guild?"

Pavicious cocked his head. "Well, it would be a shame to lose you, but I would recommend you find a different city to work in. I remove my enemies much more efficiently than Spot."

Kaisha leaned close to Ryshander's ear. "Let's do it, my love. Would the captain have come to our aid? I think not.

This is what we have been looking for."

Ryshander nodded. "Ok, Pavicious. We will entertain your idea. What's next?"

Pav-co smiled. "Meet one of my men in the alley behind the Blue Dragon Inn tomorrow night at dusk. I'll show you to your new home. I'm sure you will be impressed."

* * *

Kellacun staggered into Soranna's cellar. She was tired and had lost a lot of blood. The old woman glanced her way and continued to water her plants. "Well, you made it back child. Squish many bees?"

Kellacun closed the door weakly and leaned on the table. "Several."

Soranna finished watering her plants and poured the rest of the water into a copper kettle. She channeled thin blue weaves of evocation and heated the water. "Looks like you were stung pretty good too."

Kellacun glanced down at the wound. It had healed much since she left the alley. "Yea. Stung me pretty good.

Can you fix this?"

Soranna opened the cabinet and pulled several towels from the top shelf. She calmly set them on the stone counter next to the heating copper pot. "Yes, sit."

Kellacun began to unbuckle the straps to her armor. "I need to be more careful. It all happened so fast. I didn't see the one behind me with the spear."

Soranna folded the towels and poured the hot steamy water into it. "Here. Clean your wound with this. The water

is hot, but it will help with an infection."

"Do rat-folk get infections?"

Soranna smiled and set the copper pot back on the stone ledge. "Sweetie, you're not invincible."

Kellacun winced as she cleaned the wound with the hot towel. "So normal weapons don't really harm me much. The wounds heal very quickly. But, I can still get sick?"

"Yes. You can be poisoned, catch a disease, and can be cursed. Actually, you are more susceptible to some poisons because your wounds heal so quickly."

"And silver, it hurts me like a normal weapon."

Soranna smiled. "Yes. But be careful, if a blade has enchantments you won't be able to tell until it cuts you. It will hurt like a real blade and it won't heal right away. Just like silver."

Kellacun soaked up the blood with the towel and tossed it to the side. She grabbed another and placed it on the nearly healed wound. "I just need to be more careful. If that spear would have been enchanted, I'd be dead."

Soranna smiled and started pealing a couple of tubers. "You need practice, my dear. You can't expect to learn all you need to know in one night. Experience takes time."

"I don't have a lot of time, Soranna."

"I know, my dear. That's why I tried to dissuade you from this course."

Kellacun roughly tossed the second towel onto the table. "Really? I had no idea that fighting for justice would be easy." She said sarcastically.

Soranna hardened her tone. "Don't sass me like a child, or I will shoo you out of here like one."

Kellacun slumped her shoulders. "I'm sorry, Soranna. It was just hard tonight."

Soranna nodded. "It will get harder."

Kellacun grabbed the sword from the table and held it before her in the dim cellar light. "This sword cut through armor tonight. Cut through it like it was clay."

Soranna placed the tubers into a bowl and began to cut carrots. "Yes, you have many great tools. Your armor is like no other leather armor. It is hard like chain and light like cloth. They both will help you on your quest for vengeance."

Kellacun striped down to her small cloths. "It's not vengeance. It's justice!"

"Oh? Justice for who?"

"Justice for my mother!" Kellacun growled.

"Just your mother?"

"Justice for my father… Justice for me." Kellacun said as she trailed off into sobs. She plopped down on the chair and placed her face into her hands and cried.

Soranna set her knife down and walked over to Kellacun. She placed her hand on the young girl's shoulder, but did not say anything.

"I took a life tonight, Soranna." Kellacun said through sobs. "He begged for a mercy that I didn't have in me to give."

Soranna gently patted Kellacun's shoulder. "Child, there is no mercy to give. Nor is their justice for you, either. You are going to have to become the monster that can live with vengeance, or you must give up."

Kellacun turned her chair and buried her face into Soranna's waist as she cried. "I cannot give up. My mother's blood screams to me from the earth."

Soranna gently stroked Kellacun's hair. "Then you have no choice, child. Just understand that this war you fight will consume who you are now. When it's over, you will have nothing left."

Kellacun pulled away from Soranna's embrace and wiped her eyes. "Maybe I won't have anything left. But then, neither will they."

* * *

Pavicious stood in the large antechamber of the underground guild hall. He had stacked up old food crates and placed them up against the wall. Dozens of thuggish and spindly looking fellows mumbled to themselves in the room as they waited for Pav-co to speak. Grascon rubbed the itchy bite mark on his wrist. Pav-co told him it was the only way he could get the gift. The wry assassin had his doubts, but the odd colored gray fur that was starting to grow around the wound seemed to prove it.

"Stop fiddling with that."

Grascon pulled his sleeve down to cover the bite. "Just itches like the dickens."

"Yea, mine did too." Pavie said "No worries, it won't hurt."

Grascon itched the bite over his shirt. "So who are we waiting on?"

"Kaisha and Ryshander."

"Do you really think they'll show up?" Grascon asked.

Pavicious rubbed his chin. "If Aldon stuck around in the old barn, I think they will. Remember, they arrived to meet

Spot somewhat late."

Grascon nodded his head lightly. "The pirate in him suspects everything is a trap."

Pavicious smiled. "Yes, I saw them scoping the barn out this morning. Quite stealthy, that pair. Had it not been for my nose, I wouldn't have noticed them."

Grascon rubbed his nose and sniffed the air. He was curious when he would get to smell as many things as Pavie.

"And like a clock." Pavicious mumbled.

Grascon turned to see Aldon walking into the antechamber with Kaisha and Ryshander in tow.

Pavicious stepped onto the crates. They wobbled a bit, but his great balance allowed him to stand with ease. "Greeting everyone. Welcome to Lostos. Your new home!"

The rogues mumbled to themselves as Pavicious continued. "I want to thank you all for coming. My old guild boss, and friend, was murdered by Duke Dolin Blackhawk. The rivalry between him and I go back before the days of the coliseum."

"Why should we care about your beef with the Duke?" One man called out. Others shouted similar sentiments.

Pav-co smiled and shushed the crowd. "You shouldn't. My qualms with the Duke are mine. However, if you didn't have a hatred for him, you would not be here."

"I'm here 'cause I love money," Aldon called out.

The crowd chuckled amongst themselves and the mood lightened.

"True, a love for money is another reason to be here tonight. But, what I'm saying is, use your motivation for your personal gain. The guild will profit from your profits.

We all will."

"I heard that your old guild master had a disease that turned him into a rat." One man shouted.

"Not a disease," Pavicious countered, "But a gift. A gift that makes you immune to most injuries and increases your healing in such a rate that you can overcome being stabbed in a few hours. It allows you to jump higher, run faster, and see better than you can imagine. He passed this gift on to me."

Aldon spoke up just as Pavicious had planned. "So if your old guild boss had the gift, how did the Duke kill him?

Not to mention, how will we keep him from killing us?" "Yea!" came the shouts from the crowd.

Pavicious motioned for silence with his hands. "Fair concerns. You see, my old guild boss, Demetrin, was the only one with the gift. He worried that if he gave it out, others might use it for their own profit. He let his principles get in the way of justice."

"That ain't gonna' help us. That she-bitch wiped out Dee and his crew in a week." A woman from the crowd called out.

Pavicious smiled. "And your name would be?"

"Mirahnka," she said flatly. "And, I knew Dee. He was a skilled swordsman and that devil woman cut him down."

Pavicious smiled. "They cut me down too, but still I stand. The elf killed the normal men and teamed up with the Duke to kill Dee. But, he was just one man. How can they defeat an army of rat-folk?"

"With enchanted swords, that's how!" A man called out.

Miranhka turned back to Pavicious. "Travits raises another good point."

"Are you cowards?!" Pavicious shouted. "You sound like a bunch of sniveling belly crawlers!"

"We ain't no cowards!" They shouted from the crowd.

Miranhka stiffened. "We ain't stupid either. They wiped out Dee's crew in a week. Unless you plan on making us all rat-folk, the monsters down here will slowly clean us out even sooner."

Pav-co smiled. "Precisely. I will reward hard working members with the gift! Your speed, strength, and senses will be multiplied. You will only fear injury from silver, or enchanted blades. United, who will be able to stand against us?!"

The crowd was silent for a moment before they broke
into applause and praise. They promised death to the Duke and fantasized about riches and station.

Pavicious waited for the crowd to die down. "This morning I gave Grascon the gift. And as a show of faith, I will give two of you the gift tonight."

The crowd was uneasily silent. "Who ya' gonna' pick?" Miranhka asked.

"Two that have already made an impact to the guild. Two members that have the skill to best help the guild right now."

The crowd looked around to one another as Pav-co made his announcement. "Would Kashia and Ryshander step forward?"

Kaisha looked at Ryshander uneasily. "Are you sure about this, my love?"

Ryshander shrugged. "No, not entirely, but the rewards outweigh the risk. And if we end up moving on, it's not like they can take the gift back from us."

Kaisha nodded. "Well, they did save us from Spot."

Pavicious smiled. "Will you humbly accept this gift?"

Ryshander stepped forward. "Though we have no personal qualms with the Duke, it would be our honor to profit by harming his villainous ways."

Grascon motioned to a side room. "Come this way. Wait inside there. We will be with you shortly. Welcome to the family."

Kashia and Ryshander walked into the small room uneasily. *Family,* she thought. That sounded nice.

Pavicious turned back to the crowd. "They will not be the last. Take this to heart… To your *Severed Heart!* When you have brought me ten gold crowns from the Duke's coffer's, you can receive the gift. Now, go out and make the

murdering bastard pay!"

The crowd erupted in cheers.

* * *

The cool morning breeze gently blew in from the bare window. Duke Dolin Blackhawk gazed out over his fine city while the elf assassin, Ulsta, sat provocatively in a council chair. His city was growing ever so quickly. The coliseum was becoming a national landmark attracting citizens from all over Terrigan, not just Beykla. He had managed to drive the rogues from his city for the most part. Hiring the AlKalidians was expensive, but it had paid off. Joshua walked into the room.

"You summoned me, father?"

"Why else would you be here, boy?" Ulsta countered.

The Duke shot her an angry glare. "Watch your tongue, elf. Let me remind you that you are in my council room. Not the other way around."

Ulsta bit her bottom lip. "My apologies, your holiness."

The Duke slammed his fist down on the desk, though Ulsta seemed uninterested at best. "This may not play out like you think, elf."

Ulsta shrugged and picked at her nails with her dagger.

"How did you get that in here?" The Duke demanded.

"You were searched."

"I often hide things in places fingers cannot find."

The Duke kicked the chair. "Must I be surrounded by insolence? Perhaps I will instruct my men to use their probing fingers."

Ulsta started to reply but was interrupted by Joshua.

"Father, did you summon me for a reason?"

"Yes, Joshua," the duke said. "One of my tax wagons was hit last night. The elf tells me they killed all of the Thieves' Guild, but you could explain this."

Joshua stammered. "Umm perhaps ruffians have stepped up in their place."

"So you made sure that Demetrin's family was dead?"

"Yes, father. I told you that."

The Duke turned angrily to the elf and knocked her legs off of his desk. "See wench, you have some explaining to do." Ulsta smiled and placed her feet back up on the desk.

"Careful where your tongue takes you, Duke Blackhawk. The rogues are all dead, except for the daughter of Demetrin. The daughter that your son protected."

"My son didn't protect anyone. He went in to search for her and to kill her. He got a tip from the street of where

Demetrin's house was."

Ulsta smiled and picked at her fingernails again. "I left a hunter in that room after killing and torturing the woman.

You want to know what she said, Duke?"

Joshua interrupted. "She just withheld information, father. She cannot be trusted!"

The Duke held up his hand to stifle his son. "Yes, I'm mildly interested, elf."

Ulsta smiled. "The woman told my hunters that her daughter, Kellacun, was out with a boy. A boy that was a city guard member named Joshua."

Joshua growled and stormed toward Ulsta. "Lies!

Stories from the lips of a murderer!" "Executioner," Ulsta corrected.

"These are bold faced lies, father."

Ulsta got up from her chair and strode around the room. Her long black cadacka flowed from the outdoor breeze that pierced the lofty council room. "My dead hunter had claw and bite marks on his body that were consistent with the wounds caused on another by the wererat, Demetrin. We identified every member of the Thieves' Guild and only one transformed. It was Demetrin."

"So, Demetrin lives. You failed elf." The Duke said.

"Not exactly." Ulsta countered. "For one, his body still rots in the mass grave south of town. Two, how did Demetrin contract this curse?"

The Duke opened a cabinet and pulled out a bottle of wine and three glasses. "He contracted it when I hired a wererat from Dawson City to kill the mason rebels."

"So, in the eighteen years since his transformation, he never passed the curse onto anyone?"

"Not to my knowledge." The Duke said as he poured the three goblets.

"So it's likely that the only way he passed the curse was in a way he had no control. To his own daughter."

"That's absurd!" Joshua said. "I killed the hunter. I killed him with the dagger that you issued us!"

The Duke handed Ulsta a goblet of wine. "Seems a bit far fetched, elf."

Ulsta smiled. "You honor me to serve me with your own hand."

The Duke grumbled. "So what do you have to say about that elf? The hunter did have stab wounds on his body.

Dozens of them."

Ulsta pretended to sip the wine. "So tell me, Joshua. Where is your dagger now?"

Joshua stammered. "I… I lost it at the house."

The Duke shook his head. "You never said that
before, Joshua. Say it isn't so! Tell me you did not help
those that would murder me!"

Ulsta stood up and pointed her dagger at Joshua.
"The rat-woman killed the hunter, Duke. Killed him
with your son's dagger. She is the one that knocked off
your tax patrol. She will want vengeance for her slain
family. She will be a very dangerous foe."

Joshua slumped down in one of the council chairs as
Ulsta continued. "She is most likely born with the rat
curse. She will be twice as strong and three times as fast
as her father. She will come for you, Duke. Are you
going to trust your family to protect you, or do you
want to work out something with me?"

The Duke slapped his wine across the room. "What
have you done? My own son has set a murderer upon
me!

And for what? A little quim!?"

Joshua stood from the chair. "You're the one that
poured oil in the bee's nest. Not me. You're the one that
started this whole thing. Had you just paid the masons
like you agreed, none of this would have ever
happened."

The Duke shook his fist. "You ungrateful little
whelp! I inherited a city in debt, a spoiled noble woman
for a wife with a baby. If I didn't turn things around,
you would be a thatcher or a smith."

"So you murdered people for me, father? How
pathetic." "So what, Joshua? You would fashion a noose
for me? Fashion one forged out of your own loin's
desire?"

"You don't understand, father. She is not like them. She is a good woman. She is innocent and I love her." Ulsta chortled and covered her mouth.

Joshua pointed at the elf. "You would mock an emotion that you will never understand, murderer. You are the pathetic one!"

The Duke pulled a piece of parchment from under the table. He opened it and dabbed a quill into ink. "This is an arrest dead or alive warrant, Ulsta."

"Father you can't! She is innocent."

"Was innocent." Duke Blackhawk corrected. "She murdered a tax patrolmen in cold blood. She is innocent no longer."

Joshua fell back stunned. Kellacun would never murder anyone.

"I want you to find Kellacun, and bring her to me. Dead or alive."

Ulsta smiled and accepted the warrant. "I will find the girl and drag her corpse before you by the end of the week." *Not if I find her first,* Joshua thought to himself.

7
Establishing the Streets

"Hurry up!" Travits yelled. "The guards will be here any minute!"

Miranhka shook her head. "Settle down. We have plenty of time."

Travits glanced out of the general store window and then back to the owner. He was face down on the floor and the pool of blood under him was growing larger. "You didn't kill him, did you? Pavie said no deaths."

Miranhka finished dumping the coins from the lock box into a small bag. "Who gives an orc shit? We got the coins. Plus, what makes you think Pavie didn't want any deaths?"

Travits glanced back at the store owner. The rogue could still see his chest rising and falling. "There just ain't no reason to kill him if we don't have to. This ain't no city business."

"Says who?" Miranhka stuffed a few extra items into her knapsack.

"Think about it. If word gets around we kill everyone, store owners will be more inclined to fight back. Jobs will get harder and I still have not earned my skins yet."

Miranhka chuckled. The term 'Earning Skins' had become slang for getting the gift from Pav-co. She had earned it last weak. "Don't be a tunthis"

Travits chuckled as he stuffed some dried meat into his pack. Being likened to a feline made him laugh quietly. Especially when done so by a rat person. "Are the others done upstairs?"

Miranhka cocked her head and the smiled faded from her face. "Let's go, we have trouble."

The pair bounced up the side stairs. Miranhka took three at a time while Travits struggled to keep up. They rounded the corner in time to see a woman in a black leather outfit burst through the window. She was wielding a silver cutlass and thrust it into Heward.

"Kellacun!" Miranhka called out.

* * *

Kellacun had been patrolling the streets for several weeks. Pavicious's men had increased the frequency of when they hit a business. She was not concerned, they had always struck at the Duke's personal affairs.

Kellacun bit into a juicy apple as she sat on the ledge of a Central City housing structure. There were dozens of these throughout the city. Some called them apartment flats. She chewed slowly and listened to the sounds of families as the washed up for the night or prepared supper. Her thoughts drifted back to when she washed up for supper or the long walks home she took with Joshua. Kellacun wiped the water from her eyes and her nose twitched. She seemed to do that when she was upset or angry. It never happened before, so she assumed it had something to do with the new found abilities.

Kellacun tossed the chewed apple core down into the alley. Her keen vision watched it break apart on the cobblestone floor. With Pav-co's crew hitting the Duke and the tax wagons as well, she was finding she was having less and less to do at night. She tried to sneak into the palace a few nights ago, but the increased attacks had caused more security and she just could not get in. But, she would make the Duke pay. Sooner or later, she would have his blood on her blade.

Kellacun started to get up when she noticed the general store across the street had not closed up yet. It was not tax day, so there was no reason that the owner should still be inside. She leaned to the edge of the roof and narrowed her bright blue eyes. She could see several figures moving around in the upstairs. The general store owner was an old widower. He would not have anyone upstairs.

Kellacun glanced down to the street. There were two fellows sitting on some crates at the edge of the alley next to the store. *Lookouts,* she thought to herself.

Kellacun leaped down from the roof and landed on the window sill of the adjacent building. She deftly shifted her weight and jumped again. She silently landed in the alley and made her way across the street. She had to be careful so the lookouts did not see her.

She quickly made her way to the south side of the street and started heading her way east, towards the general store. The alleys were bare, save for a few barrels of refuse or a token drunkard. Kellacun spotted a sewer grate that had been left open. She peered down inside. She could see the moss on the iron rungs was disturbed. She smiled as she now understood why she was unable to find where Pavicious was holed up. Kellacun entertained the idea of somehow obstructing the passage, but she was more concerned on helping the elderly shop owner.

Kellacun made her away around the side of the building and silently approached the two lookouts. She could smell the weapon oil from their blades. She encroached ever so slowly. Like a python before the strike.

"Wish they would hurry up." One lookout said.

"Yea, but it is an easy three silver. Sit and keep guard."

The first lookout chuckled to himself. "Yea, but I need another three gold to earn my skins. I ain't gonna' get them sittin' on my ass in this alley."

Kellacun slowly drew her sword as she stalked forward. She let the rage over take her. Her body quivered and shook as her sallow skin was soon covered in black fur. Her fingernails elongated and in seconds, she was in her rat form. She wanted to call out to the men. Tell them to throw down their weapons, but that would only alert those inside. She had no choice. She had to dispatch them quickly.

Kellacun stabbed forward with her cutlass. The enchanted blade neatly pierced the body of the first lookout as she grabbed the other by the hair. She ripped his head back and her sharp rat teeth bit down on his neck. She could taste the warm coppery blood erupt into her mouth. The

first lookout struggled against her cutlass, but the shock of the wound toppled him forward. She let go of her sword and gripped the second even tighter. She fell on top of him as she shook her head, ripping more flesh away from the dying man. He tried to call out, but he could only gurgle in protest as he quickly bled to death.

Kellacun roughly tossed the bodies back into the alley. She sheathed her sword and scampered up the guttering of the general store. She paused at the second story and peered in, allowing her rat form to fade away. There were two thieves in the upstairs, stuffing valuables into bags. She did not see any sign of the old shopkeeper. She silently slid open the window and stepped in. She could smell the rogues sweat and weapon oil. But she smelled something else. It was fresh blood. Not the blood that was on her, but similar. It was the smell that Soranna told her about… The smell of another lycanthrope. It did not come from the two men, it came from downstairs. Kellacun drew her cutlass and stepped forward. She could hear people rushing up the stairs. She had to act fast.

With a single leap, Kellacun propelled herself ahead and thrust her blade into one of the men. He arched his back in pain and fell dead. Just as she pulled her blade free, the door burst open.

"Kellacun!" Miranhka called out.

Kellacun could smell the stink of the rat on her. It was strong. She had not been cursed long. "What are you doing here? I told Pav-co I would kill any of his men that strayed from the duke's marks."

"Go! Get out of here," Miranhka called out. "I will deal with her."

"Tell me where the old man is, and I will let you live." Kellacun growled.

Miranhka smiled and circled Kellacun. "He's alive. At least the last time I checked."

Kellacun forced the circle so she could maneuver downstairs. "I have killed three of your crew. Mess with another helpless citizen and I will kill the lot of you."

"You don't own the streets, bitch. Pav-co does."

Kellacun narrowed her blue eyes. "Then go and tell your fat master, what I have said."

Miranhka could feel the deadly confidence in Kellacun's voice. She wanted to strike her dead, but she knew Pavco would be angry if she did. "It's your lucky day, bitch,"

Miranhka taunted. "I'll let you live."

Kellacun watched her leap from the window. She immediately turned and started down the stairs. When she reached the bottom, she was angry she did not kill Miranhka. The entire shop had been ransacked. She moved around the corner of the counter and she found the old shop keeper. He had suffered a blow to the head. Kellacun gently turned him over, but she was too late. He was dead. Kellacun tried her best to count how much damage had been done and how much had been stolen. She would extract that value on Pav-co and his men. They would pay for this.

Kellacun started up the stairs when the front door of the store burst open. She turned to see several city militia. They were wearing the leather armor and their flowing red silk capes. She ignored their commands to stop and easily avoided their poorly aimed crossbow bolts as she bounded up the stairs. When she reached the roof, she paused and took in the scene. The old shop keeper was murdered and the city guards were unable to do anything about it. Kellacun steeled herself before disappearing into the night. If there was no justice in this city, she would have to be the one to bring it to bear.

* * *

The sound of hammers ringing on steel and stone echoed through the Lostos Guildhall. Workers-turnedrogues littered the underground complex, repairing and engineering the once underground palace into a fortress.

Pavicious watched over some engineers that were installing an elaborate hoisting platform in his private chambers. The chubby thief planned on using it for an emergency escape in the rare event his guildhall was compromised.

Grascon entered the chamber and smiled, admiring the masonry and work being completed out in the hall. "The coffers are filling up, rapidly."

"Good." Pavicious said with a smile. "How did the runs go last night?"

Grascon's smile faded. "Not so good."

"Oh?"

"We lost three to the elf."

Pavicious kicked over a bucket of tools. "Damn! That is six this week. We only recruited four."

"The men are getting nervous and profits have dropped." Pavicious nodded as he rubbed his chin. "I know. That's why I ordered Miranhka to hit outside of the Duke's controlled businesses."

Grascon narrowed his eyes. "Is that a wise move? Surely we risk running into guild member's friends and relatives."

"True." Pavicious said. "But, I checked this one out. It is an old widower near the south side of town. No relation or friends to any of us."

Grascon shook his head lightly. "Still, he likely has some kin that will be angry. It is one thing to hit our enemy's purse, but to create enemy's only makes the Duke stronger."

Pav-co smiled and placed his arm on Grascon's shoulder. "I am way ahead of you, my friend. You see, if it comes back to us, we will blame the attack on murderers.

Unlike us."

"Murderers?" Grascon asked.

"Yes, you see, we have never killed anyone other than guards when we attack. So we create an invisible foe. We then extort money from shop owners to protect them against the fake murderers."

Grascon smiled. "So we will be taxing businesses to protect them from us. But they think it's from someone else."

"Exactly. Not to mention, if they don't, they are counting on the Duke to protect them, and we hit those.

Soon, they will rebel against the Duke… Increasing our profit and decreasing his power."

Grascon nodded his head. "My friend, you're a genius. If you were an attractive bar maid, I would kiss you right on the mouth."

Pavicious laughed. "We still have Kellacun as the wild card. She could cause us a lot of harm. We need to get her to

join the guild or kill her outright."

Grascon nodded. "I agree. She's been helping somewhat. She has been hitting the tax patrols as well."

"Yes, she is surely getting rich by now." Pavicious said.

"It's time to offer her a place here in the hall."

"Getting rich?" Grascon said. "No, you misunderstand your informants. She has been giving the money back to the peasants."

"What!?" Pavicious snarled. "She has been giving it back? All of it?"

Grascon nodded. "So our reports go."

"That's not all she is doing." Miranhka said as she strolled into the hall.

Pavicious turned and took her in. She was a ravaging beauty. She had long dark hair and dark skin. Had she been taller, he would have taken her for a Kai-Harkian.

Miranhka smiled knowingly at Pavicious. She did not have to turn in her gold for the gift and had contracted it instead by a bite during a romantic affair with the corpulent guild leader.

"So what else has this bitch been doing?" Pavicious asked angrily.

"She killed three of our crew last night as we hit the widower's market."

"May the gods damn her!" Pav-co shouted. "I assume you killed her?"

Miranhka shook her head. "No, she killed our lookouts and then skewered Heward."

"And you did nothing?" Grascon asked.

Miranhka gave him a nasty glare. "No, I ensured our fourth man escaped with loot, and I brought in a fair sum myself. Getting killed on a job that was supposed to make money was risking too much. If we want to kill her, then we should send an assassin, not burglars. She moved incredibly fast. I think her speed and talents are beyond me."

Grascon snubbed his nose at her. "Most likely she is above you."

Miranhka ignored the insult. "On the bright side, I didn't have to pay the lookouts or split Heward's share.

Travits and I made a fair sum. You can count on that."

"Pavicious ran his hand through his thinning hair. "Did you at least kill the shop owner?"

Miranhka smiled. "Yes, I'm pretty sure he was dead. We were interrupted in the middle, but I doubt he could have survived the blow. It seems the gift has made me quite strong."

"Give the numbers to Myles and he will pay you."

Miranhka smiled and bowed before she left. "Yes, my lord."

"So now what?" Grascon asked.

Pavicious shook his head as he rubbed his chin. "Dee would roll over in his grave if he knew what Kellacun was doing."

"You mean the open pit his body rotted in?"

Pavicious chuckled. "Yea, I guess he has plenty of room. Ok, let's do this. Send Ryshander and Kaisha to speak with her. Tell them that if they can convince her to join, great. If not, they're to kill her."

Grascon nodded. "Ryshander is a skilled swordsman as well as Kaisha. With both of them having the gift, I bet they could rival the elf all by themselves. Kellacun will have to join."

Pavicious shook his head slightly. "No, I think the bitch will make them kill her. She is a lot like her father in that right."

* * *

"You see her?" Kashia asked as she and Ryshander scanned the streets from the rooftops.

"No."

"I don't like this, my love."

Ryshander sighed and turned to Kaisha. "I don't either, but there are going to be several things we don't like. Look at how much money we have earned. We can soon buy our own wedding rings. In a few years, we should make enough
to buy our own cottage and retire."

Kaisha smiled as her almond orbs locked onto Ryshander's. "I love you," she said softly.

Ryshander smiled back. "I don't know this woman, but, she is threatening our future."

Kaisha nodded. "I know, but killing her is wrong."

"Okay, my love. We won't kill her. We will tell Pavco she got away."

Kaisha smiled and stroked his cheek. "I love you." The two were interrupted by a shriek in the night.

"What was that?" Kaisha asked.

"It was a woman. We need to get over there. Maybe Kellacun is not as good of a person as we thought."

The pair erupted from their perch and deftly scaled the gutter spout down to the street. "This way." Kaisha called out as they darted through the alleys.

When they rounded the corner they saw a woman laying on the ground. She had her blouse torn open, exposing her breasts. A young boy, maybe ten years old, stood in front of two men. They were laughing and taunting him.

"Come on, boy. We won't hurt yer' momma. We just want to spend a little time with her. A woman of her stature could nourish us all with those bosoms."

The other man laughed. "He's angry 'cause he still suckles."

The woman sat up and covered her bare breasts with her hands. "Please, do with me what you will. But, I need that money. It's going to send my son to the academy in Westvon."

The men laughed. "Westvon? That uppity church academy for the holy rollers?"

Kaisha signed to Ryshander. They had spent many hours perfecting Pavicious's underground signs. "These are Pavicious's men. I know the one on the left is named Hartwan."

Ryshander nodded and signed back. "Okay, let's get back to our task."

"What?" Kaisha signed furiously. "We can't let them rape and steal from this woman."

"Yes we can. Interfering is not going to win us favor with the guild. We need to pay our dues and get out."

The boy stepped towards the men. His hand trembled as he held the dagger. "You get. Or I'll stick ya' good. You ain't hurting my mom."

The men laughed and feigned fear. "Ooooo he's a tough one, ain't he, Hartwan?"

Hartwan held his belly and laughed.

"My daddy ran off with a tramp. That makes me man of the house." The boy said. "Now give my mom her money back, or I will call on the strength of Stephanis and run you through."

Hartwan stuck his chin out and leaned forward. "Yer' daddy ran out on yer' momma? Why? She's such a tasty little strumpet. I bet she wouldn't swallow her tube steak like a good woman should."

The other rogue nearly fell over with laughter. "She's gonna' swallow ours, that's fer' sure. Now get boy."

"In the name of Stephanis!" The boy lashed out. The sharp dagger caught Hartwan under the chin and sliced a deep gash under his neck. He grabbed his throat and gurgled as hot red blood erupted from the wound.

The second rogue grabbed the boy's wrist and punched him in the side of the head. The boy fell to the alley floor. He stifled his cries, but tears streamed down his puffy cheeks.

Kaisha had seen enough. She erupted from the darkness and plunged her rapier into the groin of the rogue. He screamed in pain and fell to the alley floor.

Ryshander signed and rolled his eyes. He loved Kaisha, but sometimes she was too emotional.

"Apollisian!" The woman called out. "Come to me."

The boy picked up his knife and ran to his mother. Tears streamed down his face as she held him close.

"You bitch!" The rogue screamed. "Pavicious will have your head."

"Who is going to tell him?" She snarled as she plunged her sword into the rogue's heart.

Ryshander sniffed the two dead rogues. "Not gifted. Regular punks."

Kaisha nodded and turned to the woman and child. "Are you two okay?"

The woman nodded. "Please, I need the money they took from me. My husband ran off chasing a whore and I have sold most of our farm to send my son to the academy in Westvon."

Kaisha nodded and began to search the dead men.

"Westvon? The religious academy?" Ryshander asked.

The woman nodded as she struggled to cover her breasts. "Yes, the Holy House of Stephanis."

Ryshander laughed. "Why send him there? The gods don't intervene in this world."

The boy nodded as he wiped the tears from his face. "Yes they do, sir. At least my god does."

Ryshander removed his cloak and handed it to the woman so she could cover herself. He kneeled down to the boy. "Oh, and who is your god, my little warrior?"

"Stephanis."

"And what is your name?"

The boy lifted his head proudly. "I am the son of Havrion Trinidy Lampara the Second. My mother calls me Apollisian. But, you can call me friend."

Ryshander smiled. "You are a brave boy. But, if Stephanis looked after you, why didn't he stop these men?"

Apollisian smiled confidently. "He did, he brought me you."

Kaisha helped the woman to her feet and handed her two bags of coins. "The first bag is yours. The second is from the good will of the people. Use it to hire workers for your farm while your son is away."

The woman smiled and wiped the new tears from her face. "Oh thank, you. May you always have Stephanis's blessing."

Apollisian struggled awkwardly to sheath his dagger and extended his hand to Ryshander. "It was a pleasure to meet you. May Stephanis always use you in the way of the light."

Kaisha pointed up the road. "There is a militia station there. They will help you secure passage from the city." The woman smiled and took her son to the streets.

Ryshander shook his head. "Apollisian."

The boy paused and turned. "Yes."

"The man's name was Hartwan. The man you killed." Apollisian looked confused and did not respond.

Ryshander nodded. "Always learn the name of men you are forced to kill. The heart has a hard time tracking numbers."

Apollisian smiled. "Those are wise words, mister. I'll remember."

Ryshander nodded as he knelt down to the dead bodies. He rummaged through their pockets, looking for hidden knives and jewelry.

"What are you doing?" Kaisha asked.

Ryshander smiled. "Well, looking for some jewelry to huck or something. If we just leave their valuables, it'll be obvious that they weren't killed for money."

Kaisha wiped the blood from her sword on one of the dead man's tunic. "Maybe the killers, were just after their purses?"

Ryshander caught a glimpse of a silhouette in the shadows. He whirled around and drew his sword. "Show yourself, lest you be cut down where you stand."

Kaisha sniffed the air. "I think it is Miranhka. A rat-folk to be sure."

They both were surprised when Kellacun stepped from the shadows.

"I saw what you did for that boy and his mother." Kellacun said.

Ryshander tensed. "So what? You gonna' inform against us to Pavicious?"

Kellacun leaned against the wall and gently stroked her silver cutlass. "Why would I do that? Because you have been trying to tail me all night?"

Kaisha stepped forward and sheathed her rapier. "So, if

you knew we were looking for you, why did you show up?" Kellacun smiled. "Because of what you did for the boy.

You're not the normal scum that Pav-co employs."

Ryshander stepped toward Kellacun again and pointed his rapier at her. "Scum? Brave words for someone who is bested in numbers and skill."

Kellacun smiled and waved her hand in dismissal. "If you really wanted me dead, you would have hunted me the right way. You would have set a trap."

Kaisha smiled and sat down on an alley crate. "Well, I suppose we could have brought in that giant cat from the
Serrin Plains."

Kellacun chuckled. "You are clearly not Pav-co's villainous scum. His men would have simply attacked another innocent store owner. They would have made sure it was on the south side of town, where I patrol the most. Instead, you are on the north side, helping poor women and their bastard children."

Ryshander did not step down. "Don't confuse Kaisha's sensitivity for weakness, fool. We come with a message. Join the guild, or we are to kill you where you stand."

Kellacun's smile faded from her face. "I don't wish to kill either of you, but if I must."

Kaisha stepped forward. "There is no need for bloodshed, my love."

"She saw us kill these two." Ryshander said as he bit his lip.

Kaisha shook her head and pushed Ryshander's sword down with her hand. "Relax, my love. Killing her won't save us from what we have done. If she joined, she could still report."

Kellacun smiled and relaxed a bit. "I know Pavicious is angry with me. I don't care. If I must, I will gut the fat pig myself. But, why not say I killed these men? We use similar weapons. Plus, I must say I enjoyed the location of the sword wound. Quite fitting for scum such as he."

Kaisha smiled. "We appreciate your willingness to take credit for the kills. We are in your debt. We will create a wild tale of your daring escape. But, know that if we must choose between your life and staying in the guild, we will reluctantly kill you. The guild is going to give us enough money to earn our new start."

Kellacun drew her cutlass and curtseyed. "I am in your debt as well. But, so we are on the same ground, I want you to know that I will kill the Duke. And as unlikely as it may seem, if you are ever in my way, I will kill you without hesitation or remorse."

Kaisha shivered at the cold blooded confidence that she could see in Kellacun's eyes. "Then I hope we are so fortunate to never cross swords with one another… For both of our sakes."

Kellacun nodded as she turned to leave.

"Kellacun," Ryshander called out.

"Yes?"

"Pav-co will send men to kill you. You know this."

Kellacun nodded. "Yes. I would be disappointed if he didn't."

Ryshander smiled. He never thought there was a woman that was as attractive as his love, but this Kellacun was surely that. He could never love someone like her.

There was something missing from her. She was cold inside.

Dead maybe.

"Let's go, my love. You have seen enough of her curves.

No need to stare as she leaves."

Ryshander flushed and smiled. "There are a million women in this world with curves, my sweets. But none of them are you."

8
Between a Rat and a Hardplace

"She what!?" Pavicious screamed as he slammed his chubby fist down on his new cherry desk. The force of the blow cracked the fine wood and splintered the polished finish.

Grascon nodded. "Kaisha and Ryshander said they were having a hard time tailing her so they called on the Johnson boys to help them."

"Damn it!" Pavicious bellowed as he kicked his ruined desk.

The workers in the room ignored his outburst and continued to sculpt and plaster the walls. The lifting platform was coming along nicely. The engineers had completed it and now the workers were just working on concealing it in the wall.

"You know I am skilled in the ways of hunting men." Grascon offered.

Pavicious nodded. "Yes, I know. I don't suppose that you would want to do this pro bono?"

Grascon shook his head from side to side. "Nope. She is too skilled. I would need double my normal rate."

Pavicious sighed and pulled on the center desk drawer. It was stuck from the damage he had caused. He pulled harder and the drawer popped open, sending papers and loose coins flying onto the floor.

"Son of an orc!" Pavicious screamed.

Grascon smiled and sat down in the plush velvety chair that was in front of Pavicious's desk. "I will need an expense account as well."

"What!?" Pavicious moaned. "What for?"

"She is fleet footed as well as deadly. I need to hire scouts, spies, and lookouts to mark her locations. I will need to pay off guards and hire a goon squad as well."

Pavicious pinched the bridge of his nose and shook his head. "You had better not fail me, Grascon. Not for this much gold."

Grascon folded his arms under his chest and leaned back in the chair. He stroked his shaggy beard in victory. "Just give me a complete moon cycle and I will have her head before you."

Pavicious narrowed his eyes. "If I write this up, you have thirty days to deliver her head, or I will have yours."

* * *

Kellacun stared blankly at the letter. It was written in an odd flowing script.

Soranna,

You have stirred up a fair amount of trouble in this fine city. Aside from helping the outlaw Demetrin on his exploits over the years, you have now aided and abetted the murderer known as, Kellacun. I have evidence that you are keeping the girl in your cellar flat. She is to come to the Blue Dragon Inn common room tonight at twilight to be arrested. If you fail to convince her to come or she comes armed, I will order a death warrant for you both.

-Duke Dolin Blackhawk

"I am sorry, Soranna."

Soranna smiled. "No worries, my child."

Kellacun felt her nose burn and fought back tears. "They know I'm here. The letter plainly says that. If I don't go to
meet them, then you'll be in danger."

Soranna sipped some tea. "Kellacun, my sweet little honey bee. Are you so daft? Do you think I didn't know what I was getting into by helping you? Do you think I did not mourn the deaths of your parents?"

Kellacun dropped the letter on the table and put her head in her hands. "You are all I have left. I can't let them take you too."

Soranna smiled and sipped her tea. "Drink some tea child. They don't want you to come."

"But the letter says they do."

Soranna chuckled. "Child, you are so refreshing. They *want* me to show you the letter. They don't want you to come. And if you do, they will likely kill you anyway." "And you?" Kellacun asked.

"Oh, they will surely kill me."

Kellacun sobbed. "Then what are we to do?"

Soranna smiled. "Go to the inn. Go armed and fight them. I will remain here. I have placed several magical wards that will keep me until the morning."

Kellacun rushed over and embraced Soranna. "I will not fail, Soranna."

Soranna reluctantly placed her hand on Kellacun's shoulder. "There child. Go to them."

Kellacun nodded. She quietly began to don her armor.

"I will bring back their heads."

Soranna chuckled. "Just stay alive. If you kill anyone, just leave their heads. I find they rot quickly and their faces will not compliment my décor."

Kellacun chuckled as she wiped a tear from her cheek.

"I'll be back."

"I know, child."

Kellacun sheathed her sword and gave Soranna a final hug. She did not look back as she left the cellar flat. The cool evening air greeted her as she strode in to the ally. She felt a finality to her life. Stepping from the warm confines of the cellar flat to the cool dark alley seemed to be the end of a life change.

The walk to the inn was one of reflection and trepidation. She did not know what she was going to face.

How many guards would there be? Would they really try to kill her? They surely would have silver weapons. They had issued them to the guards long before she knew of her talents. Ultimately, it did not matter. She would have to deal with whatever was there. She had little choice.

* * *

"Grascon," the guard panted as he placed his hands on his knees.

Grascon looked up from his plate of food. "What is it?"

The guard held his chest. "I have something you might want to know about Kellacun."

Grascon frowned. "Then sit, fool. Get a flagon and relax. Your panting and heaving is only going to spread our business all over the bar."

The guard reluctantly sat down. He ordered a drink and glanced nervously about the room. "I could get hung for talking to you."

Grascon nodded as he shoveled a spoonful of baked tubers into his mouth. "Yes, but you could earn a year's wage as well."

The guard nodded and took a long draw from the flagon the wench served. "I know where Kellacun is going to be tonight."

Grascon stopped chewing and smiled. He swallowed his bite and took a drink. "Good. How much for this information?"

The guard fiddled with his mug nervously. "Ten gold."

"You asking for ten, or telling me it will cost ten?"

The guard swallowed hard. "Telling."

Grascon smiled. "Ok. Ten it is."

The guard nodded and leaned in. "She is to be executed at the Blue Dragon Inn at twilight."

Grascon nearly spit out his drink. "That's now!"

The guard nodded. "I know. That's why I was in such a hurry."

Grascon quickly opened his coin purse and started counting coins. "Did they catch her? Why there?"

"The elf bitch found out she was living with an old seer named Soranna. They arranged for Kellacun to turn herself in tonight, or they would kill them both. Cept'in they plan on doing that anyway."

Grascon tossed ten gold coins on the table. "Obviously." The guard quickly scooped up the coins.

"There is another gold coin in this for you if you will do one more thing."

The guard smiled wide with greed. "And that is?"

Grascon slid his cloak over his shoulders. "Don't tell any of my other informants you talked to me. Keep this our secret."

The guard frowned in confusion. "But don't you want help killing Kellacun in case the elf fails?"

Grascon smiled. "I will have things well under control."

* * *

Kellacun reached down for the door and paused. The gentle night air blew her dark cloak around her form.

"You going in, or what?" a gruff voice growled.

Kellacun stepped to the side. "Sorry."

"No problem, ma'am. Didn't mean to upset you. Thought you were a drunkard like me."

Kellacun smiled sheepishly at the large man. He was balding and a bit chubby. His hands were calloused from field work. Kellacun noticed she watched hands a lot as of late. "It's okay, I'm waiting for a friend."

"Might as well wait inside. It's a bit draft out here."

Kellacun nodded nervously. She knew once she stepped inside, there was no going back. Part of her wanted to turn around and run.

"Come on, then. I'll buy ya' a drink."

Kellacun smiled warmly. Despite this man's appearance, she felt comfort in his voice. "Okay," she said.

Kellacun followed the man inside the common room. As soon as she cleared the door, she could feel the tension in the air. The tables had been cleared to the side, making an odd open area. The patrons were sitting to the far south of the room, near the stage. Kellacun followed the man to the bar. She placed her elbows on the polished wood and leaned forward. She tried to steal a glance to the room, but was unable to see anything out of the ordinary.

"I need an ale for me, and something fer' ma' friend."

The barkeep adjusted his eye patch as he wiped down the counter. "Yer' wife know about yer' strumpet?"

"Stuff it, Zeke." The man said. "She ain't no strumpet of mine. Just get our damn drinks."

The barkeep smirked and set two wooden flagons on the bar. He grabbed one and filled it from a wooden keg behind him. When it was full, he set the drink on the counter. "What do you want, missy?"

Kellacun tried to look behind her as she answered. "I'll take an ale as well."

The barkeep filled the mug and slid it back. "That'll be two copper or ten wood."

The man tossed a handful of wooden tokens on the bar and turned around to appraise the room. He took a long draw and sighed. "Now that hits the spot."

Kellacun sipped her ale. "Tell me what you see. Do you see any guards?"

The man frowned. "Nope. No guards here."

"Are you sure?"

The man frowned. "No guards, lady. You wanted or something."

Kellacun sighed with relief. "Something like that."

The barkeep lowered his head. "Holy shit. Yer' Dee's girl. You come out to play?"

Kellacun removed the hood from her cloak. Her long black hair fell down to her shoulders. "What do you mean, play?"

"I mean that Dee has a lot of enemies around here."

Kellacun sipped her ale. "I don't want any trouble."

A small figure stepped from the crowd. She had long flowing silver hair and was adorned in a black cloak with silver runes dancing down the edges of it. "Well, that's disappointing." the small woman said. "I am surely looking for some trouble."

Kellacun turned to see a small female elf. She was barely five foot tall. She wielded two thin oddly shaped swords over her back. Behind her stood four massive men. They had bright brass colored helms shaped like skulls with the horns facing forward. Kellacun immediately recognized them as hunters. She had managed to kill one, but now there were four. Kellacun felt her body begin to rage with anger and fear. Part of her wanted to run, and the other part wanted to draw her sword and rush in. Was this the elf assassin that killed her family? How could she fight the elf and the hunters at the same time? Soranna was right, she would fail.

Glazric, the half-orc bouncer, stepped forward. He was every bit as tall and more muscular than the hunters. "If you're looking for trouble, look for it outside, wench."

Ulsta stepped forward. "There is no need to look outside, pigger. I found it here. Now, unless you want to be a victim of my blade I suggest you take yer' coward pig ass over there and sit down."

Glazric growled at the racial slur. Orcs were often referred to as having pig noses. To be called a pigger was a gross insult for a half breed. The bouncer tightened his fist and reached for his cudgel.

"Stand down, Glazric." The barkeep demanded. "This is not yer' fight."

* * *

Joshua pulled his cloak tight as he roamed the streets. Something was going on tonight at one of the inns. He had heard his father talking about it last night with the elf bitch. He knew it had to be an ambush for Kellacun. There were seven inns in the Central City. If he hurried, maybe he could find her in time.

* * *

Kellacun knew she could not run. The blood of her parents screamed at her for justice while her soul screamed for vengeance. Kellacun casually unfastened her cloak clasp and let it fall to the floor. "You're the bitch that killed that my parents."

Ulsta smiled and curtseyed. "I admit it with pride."

Kellacun narrowed her eyes. Her fear was replaced with unbridled rage. She could feel her feral form clawing to get from her. "I will pick up where my father left off. Except, I will kill you."

Ulsta smiled. "I would say you would die like your father, but I would liken your abilities more to your pathetic mother."

"You will bleed for that, bitch!" Kellacun screamed as she drew her sword and rushed forward.

Bar patrons gasped and scrambled to get to the far end of the bar as the hunters sprung to life.

Kellacun grunted as the weight of the first hunter hit her in the side. The force of the blow carried them into the bar. Their bodies crashed into it and sent showers of wood across the common room. Ulsta stabbed her twin swords into the floor of the inn and smiled. She sat down at a nearby table and gently sipped wine from a crystal goblet.

"What the!?" The barkeep screamed. "Glazic, end this nonsense!"

Glazric grabbed his cudgel and stepped forward. One of the hunters drew his axe and stepped in front of Glazric. The two mighty men stood face to face. The hunter shook his head from side to side as the fight raged on behind him.

Kellacun smelled the feral odor on this hunter and it was the same as the one she fought in her home. It had some property about it, something unnatural. The odor sent a rage through her. She felt her strength surge. As the hunter squeezed her neck with his powerful arms, Kellacun shifted her weight. She grabbed the hunter by his belt and fought to her feet. With a mighty roar she leapt into the air. Bits of wood and debris that had been on top of them exploded in all directions. Kellacun rammed the hunter into the thick wooden rafter of the ceiling. The beam splintered under the force of the blow. Kellacun drew her cutlass and with a swift slice, she severed the head of the large man. Blood erupted from the wound as the head bounced and tumbled to the feet of the elf. Kellacun shook her head to readjust her hair. "One down, three to go."

Ulsta slammed her goblet down. Wine splashed on the table. "Kill that bitch! Now!"

The second hunter standing next to Ulsta sprung to life and rushed forward. His heavy footfalls thundered across the common room floor.

* * *

"Kellacun, lookout!" Glazric snarled and brought his heavy cudgel down on the head of the hunter. The thick wooden stock splintered as it knocked the monster's head to the side. The beast turned and faced the half-orc. Glazric glanced down at his shattered beatstick in astonishment.

The hunter chuckled deeply and brought his axe down. Glazric recovered quickly and caught the deadly weapon by the haft. The hunter shoved forward and slammed the half-orc against the wall. The shelves shuddered and picture frames fell to the floor. Glazric struggled against the titanic strength of the hunter. The monster reached down and grabbed Glazric by the belt. He shifted his legs under him and hoisted the astonished half-orc into the air. With a mighty heave, Glazric was tossed over the bar. His wide back crashed into shelves containing bottles of wine and strong spirits. The bouncer fell to the floor behind the bar and was covered with the broken bottles and their contents.

The hunter leapt to the top of the bar. He crouched low and smiled. Glazric lay stunned on the floor. As the wounded half-orc tried to stand, the hunter steadied himself and reared back with his deadly axe.

A patron next to the fight lunged in with his sword. The thin blade neatly pierced the hunter's calf. "Come on, Glaz!

Get up!"

The hunter peered down and looked at the blade that was stabbed into his right leg. He followed it up to the astonished look of the patron. The beast reached out and grabbed the small man by the wrist. In a quick fell motion he twisted and shattered his arm. The man screamed and grabbed at the iron like grip as he tried to free himself. The hunter started to swing his axe when Glazric stood up from behind the bar. He grabbed the monster's horned helm. The half-orc flexed his powerful shoulders and ripped the hunter down. The maniacal beast fell behind the bar and landed on his axe. The razor sharp blade ripped through the beast's chest.

Glazric ignored the shards of broken glass sticking out of his shoulder and his back. He gingerly moved to the patron that had saved his life. "Are you okay?"

The patron smiled weakly as he cradled his shattered forearm. It hung limp at an unnatural position. "It will heal,

I think."

Glazric smiled and turned back to see if Kellacun was ok.

* * *

The remaining two hunters charged. Kellacun backed herself against the wall and crouched low. Her cutlass was stretched wide and her other hand was extended for counterbalance. She flashed her fangs and hissed. "Come to your deaths!

The two hunters rushed in. Kellacun flattened low to the floor as one of the attackers swung his axe wildly. She reached down and snatched up the first dead hunter's axe with her left hand and she stabbed in with her right. Her razor sharp cutlass smoothly pierced the hunter's side.

The second hunter lunged in with his axe. Kellacun leaned sideways and leapt onto the bar as the first attacker sliced in. His axe stuck neatly into the wood counter just between her legs. She cart wheeled over the axe without using her hands. She brought the hunter's blade across in a swinging motion. The weapon severed the hunter's arm at the elbow as it still gripped the axe that was lodged in the bar. The bloodied blade fell from Kellacun's grasp.

The hunter ignored the blood pouring from his severed limb and punched at her. She leaped over him and twisted in the air, bringing her cutlass down into the head of the first. With both hands gripping her sword, she forced the enchanted blade through the brass helm and deep into the hunter's skull. Blood and gore erupted from the wound as the hunter fell lifeless to the floor.

Kellacun wrenched her sword free and stabbed backwards as she kept her eyes fixed on the elf sitting at the table. The cutlass pierced the wounded hunter in the throat. Kellacun did not turn as her keen ears caught the hunter's dying gurgled protests.

"Your reign of terror will soon be at an end." Kellacun growled.

* * *

Glazric caught movement out of the corner of his eye. He turned to see the wounded hunter standing. His own axe was stuck in his chest and he held the small thin sword the patron had stabbed him with. Blood poured from the wound in his chest, but the beast of a man did not seem to notice. "Want some more?" Glazric taunted.

The hunter lunged in weakly with the sword. Glazric stepped to the side and grabbed the hunter's wrist. The half-orc rammed his fist into the inside of the monster's arm and forced the thin sword up into the hunter's chin. The slender blade pierced the soft flesh in the monster's neck and wedged itself hilt deep to the beast's chin. Glazric was amazed when the hunter grabbed his wrists and tried to force the blade from his hands. The half-orc could tell the monster was weak.

Glazric groaned and hoisted the hunter into the air. He twisted his weight and rammed the beast into the dragon skull that hung into the common room wall. The deep azure horn erupted from the hunter's chest. The man's helm fell from his head.

"What the hell are you?" Glazric asked as he was taken aback by the man's face. It was twisted, scarred and his eyes had been sewn shut.

* * *

Ulsta shook her head and finished her wine. She tossed the goblet to the floor.

"Time for you to die, elf." Kellacun growled.

Ulsta lowered the cowl of her cloak and pulled her swords from the floor. "Looks like we are going to have to handle you ourselves."

Kellacun frowned. "We? There is only you. I have dispatched your mindless man slaves."

Ulsta smirked. "Kellacun, have you met my twin sister, Ulma?"

9
Double the Trouble

Kellacun kicked herself as she stared at the twin elf assassins. That would explain how she kept getting conflicting reports from the peasants that put the elf in different places at the same time.

A small gray elf stepped into the room from outside the inn. She looked identical to Ulsta, yet her swords were slightly different. They matched, but were thinner and shorter. She had long silver hair and she wore the same black cloak and leather armor with the silver lining that was covered in strange runes.

Ulma stepped next to Ulsta. She smiled and spoke in elven. "Don't worry about giving me back my enchanted blade. Use them both. I will use these donjuriks to distract her."

Ulsta stepped forward. "My sister and I were hired to kill every member of the wererat Thieves' Guild." She said as she pointed her sword at Kellacun. "You are the last."

Ulma smiled and drew her swords. "We are about to immortalize you, girl. Only the best enemies are allowed to be killed by the Al-Kalidian. You should be honored."

Glazric pulled the sword from the chin of the dead hunter hanging from the dragon skull. He tossed it through the air. "Kellacun, here!"

Kellacun deftly caught the blade by its handle. She flipped it up into her hand.

Ulma chuckled. "Bar room tricks are not going to save you, girl. Tonight, you draw your last breath."

Kellacun snarled as she charged in. "Then I will hold it until I have cut out your hearts!"

* * *

"I told you there had been an old woman murdered." The lead guard said as he walked next to Grascon. "The assassin Kellacun was behind it."

Grascon nodded. "Seems odd…Why would she do that?"

"How do you think the Duke got his information?" The second guard said. "The old woman informed against her."

Grascon nodded. That made sense. He was beginning to see a vindictive side of her. "So who was the old woman?"

"Who knows. It doesn't matter. We are running out of time and the Duke wants to see you."

Grascon shrugged his shoulders as they walked up the stairs to the city civic building. "We better hurry, I have a pressing engagement."

"Such as what?" The Duke slipped into an evening house coat.

Grascon smiled nervously. "Sir, the arrangement we had. I have a lead on it."

The Duke grabbed Grascon by the hair and wrenched his head to the side. "I don't have any arrangement with you, orc shit. Remember that."

Grascon winced and tried to hide his contempt. "Yes, my lord. I was referring to the arrangement you have with my boss, Pavicious."

The Duke roughly shoved his head to the side. "So what do you have to report?"

Grascon straightened his hair. "I am here to report that they are in place, as we planned."

The Duke nodded. "Good. Tell your boss that he has the flag to kill them both."

Grascon nodded. "By your leave, my lord."

Duke Blackhawk waved Grascon off and started back up the stairs. "Oh, Grascon."

"Yes?"

"Tell Pavicious that if he fails in killing them both, our deal is off."

Grascon nodded. "Consider them dead, my lord."

* * *

Kellacun panted heavily. Fighting in her wererat form had distracted the pair enough that she had managed to survive. She ignored the wounds that covered her body. Her armor had repelled many of the slashes, but the stabs had managed to cut through the tough demon skin on several occasions. The elf with the short swords was not as skilled as the one with the longer ones. Or so she thought at first.

Kellacun discovered that the elf with the short swords varied her skill with her strikes. At first this confused her, but then it began to make sense. The elf with the short swords was not wielding enchanted blades. She was nothing more than a distraction so the elf with the longer swords had the enchanted ones.

The twins rushed in. Kellacun brought her tail around and smacked Ulsta in the head. The force of the blow knocked the elf's strike wide. Ulma thrust in. Kellacun hoped she had guessed correctly with the short swords. She ignored the strike and she winced as the cold steel pierced her abdomen. She could feel the razor sharp blade slice through her insides.

Ulma tried to recover from the stunning blow, but Kellacun thrust her cutlass in. The enchanted blade sunk deep into her chest. The elf cried out and fell to the floor of the inn, clutching the sword.

The wererat grabbed Ulsta's sword arm and thrust the patron's thin blade into the elf's neck.

"Veeachei!" Ulsta gurgled. The elf ignored the thin sword and stabbed in with her second blade.

Kellacun screamed and let go of the patron's sword. She could feel the hot stinging burn of the second sword as it pierced her chest. Her vision darkened and she fell to her knees. Bright blood erupted from Ulsta's neck and sprayed out onto the common room floor.

* * *

"Why did you summon us?" Kaisha asked as she rushed through the night.

Grascon ducked around a corner and ran through the dark alleys at breakneck pace. "Because I don't trust anyone else in the guild."

Ryshander jumped over an alley crate. "You said you wanted help killing someone. We are quite capable of that."

Grascon smiled as he ran across the cobblestone street to the Blue Dragon Inn. "That's exactly why I have you with me."

* * *

Kellacun felt her lungs getting warm and heavy. She was having a hard time breathing. She coughed and spit up bright red blood on the floor. She was vaguely aware of her surroundings. She noticed that one of the elves was starting to move. The assassin knew that if she did not get to her feet soon, the second elf may kill her.

Kellacun felt an easy calm. If she died, she still killed one. She did what her father could not. She had justice for one of them. Kellacun reached down and grabbed the hilts of the elven swords that were lodged in her abdomen. If she died, she would not be able to protect Soranna. Her mind imagined the lone elf cutting down the old woman. Rage filled her. Kellacun groaned and pulled the swords free from her body.

She struggled to her feet. Her legs were numb and wobbly, but she managed to right herself. The other elf had grabbed her cutlass from her body and managed to get to her knees. Kellacun saw a group rush into the room.

"Hold!" A voice called out.

She ignored it. She would have her justice. Kellacun stretched her arms wide. Blood dripped from the blades and pooled on the floor. She could feel her wounds closing and her strength returning. "Some would say I am granting you mercy with this quick death."

Ulsta weakly lifted her head and stared into Kellacun's bright blue eyes. "Cuma sal toget, veeachei!"

"No, mercy for you, elf. I give you justice!" Kellacun screamed as she brought both swords down in a scissor motion. Ulsta's stark wide eyes starred blankly into the distance as her head bounced across the common room floor.

* * *

Grascon drew his rapier and stepped into the room. Kaisha moved in front of him.

Ryshander shook his head. "We are not killing her."

Grascon frowned. "What? Fifty gold crowns for her head."

Kaisha shook her head. "No way."

"Fifty, you say?" Ryshander said as he rubbed his chin.

"Ryshander Bradley Delone!" Kaisha growled.

Grascon frowned. "If we don't kill her, Pavicious will have her hunted down and killed anyway."

Kaisha glanced back over to Kellacun. She was leaning over a table and struggling to keep her balance.

"Move aside, if we don't do it now, we may never get another chance." Grascon said as he tried to step around them.

Ryshander sighed. "Grascon, there is honor among thieves. Kaisha is right. If you try to kill her tonight, we will stand against you now and against the guild forever."

Grascon groaned. "But look at the trouble she has caused us all."

Kaisha pointed to the dead elves. "And look what she has done for us. And think of the trouble she has caused the Duke."

Ryshander nodded. "And for that alone, she should be given a chance to flee. Would Pav-co spend thousands of gold if she fled the city?"

Grascon stroked his thin beard. "Agreed. Let's at least give her that chance."

The three walked over to Kellacun. The room was bare of patrons except for the small man that helped Glazric.

Grascon stood next to her as she weakly leaned on the table.

"I was supposed to kill you tonight."

Kellacun turned her head. Her sleek black hair fell down from her face. "What are you waiting for then."

Kaisha felt the color drain from her. This woman was different from the one they met in the alley.

Grascon bit his lip. "After talking it over with my associates, we have decided to offer you an alternative."

Kellacun glanced back to see the two lovers she had met in the alley. "So? What are you offering?"

Kaisha stepped forward. "Kellacun, you are a good person. Flee the city. Don't cross the Duke and Pav-co. If you make them enemies, they will team up against you."

Ryshander nodded. "You will not survive."

Kellacun glanced down at the twin swords sitting on the table.

"You will never reach them in time, Kellacun." Grascon said. "But you don't have to. I am leaving. But the next time we meet, we will likely be enemies. I will offer no quarter."

Ryshander helped Kellacun to the chair as Grascon stepped to the doorway. He glanced down the street to see if the guards were coming.

Kaisha rummaged through her pack and placed a small glass carafe on the table. "Those swords are likely enchanted. Drink this. If you survive your wounds, it will take months for them to heal." Kaisha offered.

Kellacun narrowed her eyes. "What is it?"

"It's a healing elixir. Ryshander has a friend on the docks that makes them."

Grascon ducked back in the bar. "Hurry up! The guards will be here soon."

Kaisha bit her lip. "We have to go. Drink this and run. Please."

Kellacun watched them hurry out the door. She weakly grabbed the elixir. The stab wounds to her body were healing fast, but the dozens of cuts to her arms and legs from the enchanted swords would take a long time to heal.

"Here," Glazric said as he placed Ulsta's two swords on the table. "You take these when you go. You earned them." Kellacun glanced up at the mighty half-orc. His bravery helped save her life. She could see he was having a hard time standing. "Sit," she said and kicked out a chair.

Glazric plopped down. "You okay, lady?"

Kellacun noticed Glazric had a deep axe wound to his back. She could smell blood on his breath. The half-orc would die soon.

"I'm ok." She said. "Drink this."

Glazric held the odd shaped bottle in his meaty hands.

"What is it?"

"It's a healing elixir. If you don't drink it, you will die."

Glazric thumbed the cork away and paused. "What about you?"

Kellacun smiled. "You are a sweet man, Glazric. Don't worry about me. My wounds are healing very fast. I'll be out of commission for a few months, but I'll be fine."

"Thought I was gonna' have to shoot them rogues." The barkeeper said.

Kellacun turned to see the barkeeper step from the stairwell. He was carrying a heavy crossbow with a silver tipped bolt head.

"You know what they are?" Kellacun asked.

"I knew Dee very well. He taught me many things. He was a good man."

Kellacun nodded.

"He would have been proud of you, Kellacun."

Kellacun fought back her tears. "I don't want pride. I want vengeance."

"Vengeance?" The barkeeper asked. "You have it. The elves are dead."

"No." Kellacun said as she stood from the table. "There is another."

The barkeeper sighed. "Careful of your path, Kellacun.

There will always be another."

"No, my friend. There will always be one until I kill him. And then there will be none." Kellacun reached into her belt pouch. "Take this gold. It will be weeks before he is able to work again. Fix up the place and hire some help." The barkeeper nodded. "If I didn't need this to repair my place, I wouldn't take it."

Kellacun smiled. "I know. If there is extra, keep it."

Glazric grinned and placed the empty elixir bottle on the table. "It was sweet. Tasted like honey nuggets." Kellacun nodded.

The barkeeper glanced outside. "I hear the guards coming. What do I tell them?"

Kellacun stood up from the table. Much of her strength had returned. "Tell them Pavicious and his men killed the elves."

"What about you?"

"Tell them I died and the guild took my body."

The barkeeper nodded as Kellacun pushed past him out the door. He reached up and grabbed her arm. "I want you to know that you have a family now. You saved me and

Glazric. We are your family."

Kellacun smiled and stroked his cheek. "No, my friend.

I died with my family months ago."

"So, are you going to leave town?" Glazric asked.

"Not as long as the Duke draws breath." Kellacun sneered. She staggered from the inn and into the silent night. Hounds bayed in the distance and she scurried away.

The adventure continues in

The Wererat's Tale
Book II: Ring of Nonul

Glossary

Ahkmentia: (ahk-men-tee-uh) Arch sucubus from the Abyss.

Aldon: (al-dun) Member of Spot's gang in Central City.

Beykla: (bey-kluh) North Eastern kingdom inTerrigan.

Bureland: (bur-land) Small hamlet in the southern part of Beykla where Lance spent most of his childhood and early adult life with his adoptive father, Davohn.

Caballus: (kab-all-us) Centar friend of the druid grove.

Casen: A type of beast that grew to unnatural size through magical corruption.

Central City: Center most city in Beykla.

Cuma sal toget: (koo-ma sal toe-get) Elven for "you are marked".

Demetrin: (duh-me-trin) Wererat leader of the thieves guild.

Donjurik: (don-jure-ick) Thin Greyshalk sword.

Dorigold: (door-eh-gold) A flower similar to dandelion.

Duke Blackhawk: Duke of Central City.

Eural Strongbow: (yur-all) Leader of a small druid frove outside of Central City.

Glazric: (glaz-rik) Bouncer at the Blue Dragon Inn in Central City.

Grascon: (grass-con) Right hand to Pavicious.

Hartwan: (heart-win) Severed Heart guild member.

Heward: (hue-word) Severed Heart guild member.

Herrazin: (herr-uh-zin) Mushrooms (like Morrelles)

Joshua: (josh-yew-uh) Son of Duke Blackhawk.

Kaisha: (kay-shuh) Lover of Ryshander.

Ka-Harkia: (kay-hark-ee-uh) Mountain counrty in the northern reaches of Terrigan.

Kahl: (call) Ancient Emperor of Tyrine.

Lostos: (low-stose) Guild hall of the Severed Heart guild.

Mara: (mer-uh) Kellacun's mother and Demetrin's wife.

Merioulus: (mare-ee-oh-you-lus) City of the gods. Set on a form of the astral plane.

Miranhka: (mir-ahnk-uh) Severed Heart guild member.

Myles: (my-uhls) Severed Heart guild accountant.

Nalir: (nal-uhr) Southern kingdom of mostly swampland.

Nonul: (non-ul) An ancient animated golem with an imprisoned soul created by elves of the Al'Kalidian.

Pavicious: (puh-viss-ee-us) Friend of Demetrin and leader of the Severed Heart guild.

Petarious Kotral Koch: (pee-tare-ee-us kaught-troll kahch) Name of the warrior transformed into Koch'Nonul.

Quasias Thinzelton: (kwaz-ee-us thin-zul-ton) A flamboyant Tengu Assassin.

Ryshander Bradley Delone: (rye-shan-dur) Pirate and Kaisha's lover.

Sinstrinian Al'Kyel: (sin-strin-ee-an al-kle-el) Al'Kalidlian elf that imprisoned Koch'Nonul's soul.

Spot: Leader of a small gang in Central City.

Soranna: (sore-ah-nuh) Kellacun's mentor.

Surshy: (sir-she) Goddess of water, and one of the four elemental gods.

Tengu: (ten-gu) Bird like assassins who can disguise themselves and mimic the voices of other humanoids.

The Torrent Inn: Inn built at the junction north of Central City and outside of the Torrent Manor.

Torrent Manor: Keep being built to the north of Central City.

Travits: (tra-vits) Severed Heart guild member.

Ulma Al-Kalidious: (ool-muh al-kuh-lid-ee-us) Grey elf assassin.

Ulsta Al-kalidious: (ool-stuh al-kuh-lid-ee-us) Grey elf assassin.

Veeachi: (vee-och-ee) Elven title for a woman with a damned soul.

Vidora: (vie-door-uh) Wild, uncivilized kingdom southwest of Tyrine that is mostly inhabited by elves.

Wererat: Creature much like a werewolf, but half rat.

About the Author

Shane Moore grew up on a farm in rural Illinois. An only child that was six miles from his nearest peer, Shane often created wild tales of heroes and villains during his many trips into the deep woods that surrounded his rural home.

Shane was accelerated in his class and started his senior year of high school at age sixteen. After graduating and getting a waiver for his age, Shane joined the United States Navy to pay for college. He participated in campaigns; "Provide Hope" and "Secure Democracy" during the Yugoslavian civil war. Shane received several naval awards and citations and was one of the highest trained members of his ship.

After getting out of the service, Shane began college. He was soon hired by the Carlinville Police Department, beginning his multiple venue police career. Shane retired as a detective for the Gillespie Police Department after serving twelve years. His police career was quite notable with awards for bravery and with one life saving medal. He was named Officer of the Year in 2005.

A lesser known truth about Shane is that he played eight years of semi Pro football with the Central Illinois Cougars. Shane is the team's all-time tackle leader and holds the record for the most special teams tackles in a season and the most tackles in a game. Shane received many awards including Defensive Player of the Year in 2005.

January 14th 2008. Shane retires from his police career to be a professional novelist.

Mr. Moore resides in Central Illinois with his wife, Tracy, and son, Dakota.